GENEVIEVE FOX COLLECTION

By Genevieve Fox

First published in 1935
Cover design by Tina DeKam
Cover art by Embla Granqvist
Illustrations by Forrest W. Orr
This unabridged version has updated grammar and spelling.
© 2019 Jenny Phillips
www.thegoodandthebeautiful.com

To R. G. F.

Contents

1. Lona Leaves Home 1
2. Lije Does His Best 9
3. Remember Amos 16
4. The Box in the Attic 19
5. Two Cakes for One Party 24
6. The Wooden Cat 31
7. Mammy Airs Her Kivers 34
8. Lona's House 40
9. The Hunt That Ended at Home 44
10. With Perfect Delight 48
11. The Coverlet Takes a Journey 54
12. Lona Tries to Write a Letter 60
13. Lona Opens a Bank Account 65
14. Lona Forgets Her Lines 68
15. To a "Furrin" Land 75
16. Homesick for Hollybush 83
17. Lona Makes a Public Appearance 88
18. Goodbye to Arden 93
19. New Furniture in the Old Cabin 97
20. Lona Aims to Help Hollybush 100
21. Santa Claus Carries a Heavy Pack 107
22. Accusations 110
23. A Busy Day 121

24. "You've Grown Up"	126
25. Two on a Hilltop	130
26. Lije Is Forgetful	135
27. A Firm Is Incorporated	142
28. Log by Log	147
29. Such a Small Pile of Logs!	152
30. The Cabins That Grew	157
31. The Working	161
32. A "Big Time" on Hollybush	166

Chapter 1

Lona Leaves Home

Lona Allen appeared to be on her way to school. She was starting down Wildcat Ridge at the usual time. She wore her school clothes—gingham dress, scarlet sweater, jaunty scarlet cap—and she carried her dinner pail. A close observer might have noticed that her great dark eyes looked feverishly bright and her cheeks unusually pink. Suspicion might have attached to the small package tucked secretively under her arm. There also seemed to be something concealed in one tightly clenched fist.

"Goodbye, Uncle Dick," she called as she went by the open door of the bare little building called the clinic, where Dick Lawrence saw the patients who came to him from up-creek and down-creek.

"Goodbye, little red-headed woodpecker," called back the surprisingly young-looking "uncle."

At the foot of the ridge, Lona waited on the Hollybush Creek trail for a girl a little younger than herself who was approaching from up-creek.

"Rachel," she said, in a solemn tone, "will you do something for me and keep still about it?"

Rachel nodded.

"You won't tell a living soul?"

"Not a soul."

"Well, I'm a-going away somewhere—fer a right-smart spell, I reckon."

"Lona Allen, what are you aiming to do?"

"Never mind what I aims to do. I jest wants to know if you'll give Aunt Sairy this letter tonight, the minute you gits home from school." With an air of great mystery, she produced a note from the front of her sweater.

"Lona, are you running away?"

"I can't tell you what I'm doing, noways. But will you promise to give Aunt Sairy the letter?"

Rachel promised.

When they came to the bend of the road at Paw-Paw Gap, Lona turned and took a last look at the little house perched high above the creek on the side of the ridge. How cheerful it looked—that "House with Many Windows," as Hollybush people called it, and how happy she had been there for almost three years. She jerked her head around and began walking so fast that Rachel could hardly keep up with her.

All the rest of the way, the conversation between the two girls was a series of questions from Rachel and of short, non-committal replies from Lona.

"But what shall I say if teacher asks me where you are at?"

"Tell the truth—that you don't know where I'm at."

At the end of nearly two hours, they reached the Hollybush schoolhouse. Reluctantly, Rachel started up the hillside path alone. "Come on, Lona," she kept saying.

But Lona shook her red-capped head stubbornly and kept going on down the stony trail toward Bull Creek.

"Don't fergit the letter," she called back anxiously.

Where Hollybush Creek joins Bull Creek stands a great rock. On this rock Lona sat down to wait for Bije, the mail carrier. Above her head, redbud bushes made gay the woods, but she did not see them. High up in the poplars, redbirds whistled and called, "Come here, come here, come here." But the sober-faced girl was deaf to their invitation.

There was none of the joy of spring in her eyes, and her forehead was wrinkled with deep vertical creases. She took the package from under her arm, refolded her nightgown, and tied it more securely. She unclenched her fist and counted over the four dollars in silver her purse contained—the earnings from crop hoeing and small chores, which she had been hoarding for two years.

"I am not a-going to school ever agin," she said out loud. "I'll burn the school down 'fore I'll go. I'm not a-going on reciting lessons with little kids and having them giggle when I make mistakes."

Lona's position was a galling one to her sensitive spirit. She was almost fourteen years old and in the third grade. Furthermore, this backwardness was not her fault. She had never been to school a day in her life until she was twelve years old. At the age when most children are in grammar school, she was reading the primer with children half her own age and laboriously learning to write her own name. And now she did examples in short division and read the third reader with eight- and nine-year-olds.

To make matters worse, Lona had become so humiliated and embarrassed by her situation that she did not do herself justice in class. No matter how well the lesson had been prepared, when she got up to recite, her wits seemed to take sudden leave of her. She was, she felt, fast becoming the class dunce and the school joke. The latter was true only in Lona's imagination, but imagined troubles are often more blighting than real troubles.

A plan had been taking form in Lona's mind for many days. This morning she had decided to carry it out. She was going to Blairstown, the coal-mining town on Big Creek, to get a job. Other Hollybush girls had gone down there and found work, she knew. Bije would be coming along soon, and he would gladly give her a ride. The rest would be simple, in her opinion.

A step sounded on the creek trail. Lona looked up to see Amos Boleyn loping along, stooped under a sack of meal.

"Howdy," he said at sight of the girl. "It's a fine-pretty mornin'."

Lona assented unenthusiastically.

"I reckon I'll rest my old legs a spell," he announced.

Lifting the bag of meal from his shoulder, he deposited it on the rock and climbed up beside Lona.

"How come you ain't in school?"

"I have something else I'm 'bliged to do." Lona's manner discouraged further questions.

"Where is it you goes to school? Is it up on Hollybush or over to the Community Center School on Slone's Creek?"

Lona wished intensely Amos would either go on home or stop talking about school.

"I've been going to Hollybush since they done built the new schoolhouse and my leg got stout. 'Fore that, I stayed over to the center and went to school."

"I recollect now. You're the little gal that had the crooked leg, and the fetched-on doctor that married our Sairy Ann Hall, he made it straight. Seemed pretty nigh a miracle." Dick Lawrence would always be the "fetched-on doctor" to Hollybush people, no matter how long he lived and practiced medicine among them. He was not a mountain man but had come from what they called "the level country" to marry Sairy Ann, a mountain girl whom he had met when she was training to be a nurse.

"Yes, Uncle Dick made me well." The girl felt a sharp twinge of remorse at the thought of the two people who meant more to her than anyone else in the world—her Uncle Dick and her Aunt Sairy Ann, as she called them. They had taken her into their home when her mammy and pappy were dead and cured her lameness and made life all over for her, and now she was running away from them.

Amos sprawled his long, blue-overalled legs out on the rock, as though he had all day before him, and looked reminiscent.

"I went to that Community School," he said.

"You!" Lona stared. Amos was past sixty, and the school was only about ten years old.

"I figured that an old man fifty-five years old didn't belong over there, but the woman from the level country, she knew I wanted book learnin' worse'n I wanted anything in this world, and she took me in. I had to go into the class with my own granddaughter, Maria, and first I thought it would kill me, recitin' with the young-uns like that. I made mistakes jest because I had such a scare on me, and sometimes I'd come out of school with my shirt all wringin' wet, and it wintertime, too. But I stuck to it for five years till I could read good and figger. And it's the best thing I ever did. As the Good Book says, 'Wisdom is better than rubies.'"

Lona fidgeted and said nothing. At last Amos raised the meal to his bony shoulders that were bowed almost into a hump from years of crop hoeing. "Well, I reckon my old woman will be a-wantin' this meal," he said and went on his way up Bull Creek, all unconscious that he had been preaching a sermon to a person who needed it.

Lona jumped down from the rock and started in the opposite direction as though someone was pursuing her. She had heard quite enough talk about school. She was going down to Blairstown to get her a job and never see the inside of a schoolhouse again. Amos could talk all he wanted to about wisdom and rubies.

It was not long before Bije's mules and "jolt wagon" came splashing and rattling up behind her.

"Whoa. Goin' fer?"

"To Blairstown."

"Git in!"

Lona climbed up over the muddy wheel and settled herself on the blanket-cushioned, springless seat. Uneasily, she waited for further questions. But Bije drove on without another word. He had the reputation for being the laziest and most silent person in the county. "Too lazy even to open his mouth, except to spit tobacco juice," was the way Pappy Hall, Sairy Ann's father, described him.

After about half an hour of jolting and rattling along without a word from Bije, Lona began to wish he would say something. She did not like being alone with her thoughts; they were uncomfortable thoughts. Her head was nearly splitting open because of the argument that was going on inside it between two Lonas.

"Amos wasn't a coward like you. He didn't run away."

"I'm not a-running away. I'm brave—going to a town where I don't know nobody and going to work."

"It's running away."

"It ain't."

Thus the battle went on under the scarlet cap. The slow, jolting ride seemed endless. At noon, Bije stopped the mules and pulled out a pail. "Got your dinner bucket?" he asked.

Lona nodded and produced her lunch. They ate in silence, then drove on. The nearer the wagon drew to Blairstown, the more Lona wished the mules were headed in the opposite direction. Panic seized her when they rounded the last bend and looked down on the dingy little town. It consisted of two rows of ugly wooden blocks that lined its one street and of stark-looking frame houses scattered over treeless and almost grassless hillsides. She had been to Blairstown once before with her Uncle Dick, but she had forgotten how dreary a place it was.

"You wouldn't know 'twas spring here," thought Lona. "It looks bare, like wintertime."

Bije relieved his mouth of tobacco juice. "Where do you aim to stay the night?"

"Why, at the hotel. I don't guess there's any other place." She remembered that there was a hotel; she and Dick had eaten an enormous dinner there.

"Miz Peek's is cheaper and safer fer a gal."

"Where's that?"

"Yonways. I'll take you over."

He drove to the end of the main street, stopped in front of a barn-like house, and left her with the stout, white-haired woman who opened the door. Halfway down the steps, Bije came back. "I'll be leavin' in the mornin', at eight o'clock sharp from the depot."

"What did he mean by that?" Lona wondered. Did he think she had just come down to do some errands? Or did he suspect that she was running away and think she might change her mind by morning? Lona never knew. She watched the mail carrier's blue-shirted back retreating down the street as a seaman marooned on a lonely island might watch a boat sailing away and leaving him to his doom.

It seemed to the girl from Hollybush Creek that Blairstown was never going to bed at all. The bright lights from the filling station across the way shone into her room till far into the night. Loud voices and loud laughter sounded in the streets. What could be going on, she wondered. For hours she twisted and turned on the bed, thinking wistfully of her little room at home on Wildcat Ridge. When she closed her eyes, she could see each of the bright-colored pictures on the wall, the homemade bed, chest of drawers and table—all of unpainted hickory wood—the cheerful patchwork quilt on the bed. How sweetly she slept there, with the murmur of Hollybush Creek in her ears. And Whitenose, her cat, was she sleeping all alone, a soft gray ball in the little box by the bed? She had occupied that box ever since she was a kitten and had come with her mistress to their new home.

Lona slept, but with sleep came a procession of dreams. She was arguing with Amos, telling him "she didn't have to go to school, nohow." But Amos kept saying over and over, "Wisdom is better than rubies. Wisdom is better than rubies." Then she was talking with Mrs. Peek, asking her when the spring would come. But that lady smiled sadly and said, "Spring don't come to Blairstown. It's always wintertime here." Thereupon Lona burst into tears and woke up to face the sober realities of a new day in a new world.

Chapter 2

Lije Does His Best

Wednesday was the busiest day of the week for Sairy Ann and Dick Lawrence. On that day, the young mothers who lived along Hollybush Creek and up its small branches and "hollers" brought their babies to the clinic. The supposed hour of this event was two o'clock in the afternoon, but the few people of Hollybush who had clocks paid little attention to them. Every week, the little procession of women and girls with bundles in their arms would begin coming up the ridge on foot and muleback a little after noon.

While Lona had been rattling along to Blairstown with Bije, her so-called aunt, Sairy Ann, had been rushing through the morning's work, cooking an early dinner for her doctor husband, her fourteen-month-old daughter Gail, and herself. Doctor Dick, in the meanwhile, had ridden to the headwaters of Hollybush to see Joe Slone, who was down with the flu, and had trotted Twinkle, his saddle horse, all the way back. As it was, they had not had time to eat half of their dinner before Mattie Boleyn walked in on them with a baby in her arms and a toddler clutching her skirt. She was followed shortly by Lizzie Gayheart with her small tribe of three and Holly Reynolds with her first baby.

"Come on down to the clinic," said Dick, swallowing a cup of coffee in two gulps and picking up his pie in his hand. He knew from experience how hard it was to get the crowd together if, as he put it, "the advance guard began roosting all over the place."

Sairy Ann left the remains of dinner on the table and changed into her nurse's uniform of spotless white. She was a graduate of a training school "down in the level country" and was an active partner with her husband in helping keep Hollybush people well. They had planned and built the little clinic together, and together they had saved many lives and relieved much misery on the creek.

"Now be a good girl, Gail," she said to the baby as she shut her up in a pen on the porch. "Here are Zipper and Pete, just waiting for you to play with them, and Granny'll be here soon."

Gail was not to be consoled by any homemade woolly lamb or gingham pup on a Wednesday, when the ridge was echoing with the voices of other babies and children. As usual, she wailed bitterly over being left behind. Why was it that her mother, usually so kind and loving, turned into a hardhearted, inhuman creature on this day?

Sairy Ann hurried to the unpainted, barn-like building just below the house. Within, it was a bright, cheerful place, in spite of its professional-looking dentist's chair, white-enameled hospital equipment, and gleaming surgical instruments. Sairy and Dick had spent hours in making the place look friendly and homelike, for Hollybush, ignorant of hospitals and modern doctors, was frightened of all these unfamiliar tools for curing sick people. A troublemaker had even set fire to the first clinic they had built, and it had burned to embers. Bright-colored pictures cut from magazines almost covered the bare board walls. The homemade benches for visitors were invitingly padded with red cambric cushions.

The long, rustic table was loaded with children's picture

books and old picture-magazines for the mothers. A crammed cupboard opened to spill out of its doors well-worn toys and other "pretties" that made the youngsters laugh with delight—toys that children in the level country had passed on to these children who had none. The "sideshows," as Sairy Ann called the books and toys, had a great deal to do with the popularity of the children's clinic.

Today the crowd broke all records. Sairy Ann could hardly get into the room to take up her post at the scales and begin weighing babies and setting down their records. Dick called out, "One at a time," till he was hoarse. There were thin babies and fat babies, pale babies and rosy-cheeked babies, three-week-old babies and toddlers. Mothers, aunts, great-aunts, and grandmothers came with them.

Long shadows were edging down the ridge toward the creek before the last visitor had started for home. "Whew-ew-cw!" whistled Dick, as he dropped wearily onto a bench. "Whew-ew-ew!" echoed Sairy. "It's a good thing Hollybush women do the milking, or they never would go home," said Dick. They sat silent for a time, too tired to move or even talk.

Suddenly Sairy Ann jumped up, went to the door, and looked anxiously from the clinic across to the house. "I don't guess Lona and Lije are home yet, and it's nearly dusky-dark." Lije was the slow-witted boy Sairy and Dick had befriended. He ran errands, hoed corn, and made himself generally useful in exchange for a loft room, his meals, and the joy of being part of that happy household at Wildcat Ridge. One of his regular duties was to ride old Whitey, the faithful family mule, down the creek and bring Lona home riding behind him.

Sairy ran across to the house. "Mammy," she called breathlessly, "have you seen anything of Lona and Lije?" Mammy Hall was sitting comfortably in the living room with Gail in her lap, telling a story. She looked forward all the week to baby-clinic afternoon, when she could have Gail to herself. Of all her grandchildren—and she had fifteen—this "least" grandchild was her favorite.

"Nary a sign of them," said Mammy.

"'Tory," begged Gail.

"I'll tell you another story next time," promised her grandmother. "I've got to git the cow milked. Maybe the teacher kept her," she suggested to Sairy as she started for her cabin up-creek.

"I hope Whitey hasn't stumbled and pitched them both into the creek again," said Sairy as she watched for a glimpse of the white mule. Whitey's legs were becoming more and more unreliable. Only a few months before, Lona had arrived home with a cut on her forehead and Lije with a sprained wrist because the elderly mule had lost her footing.

"If they aren't here in ten minutes, I'm going after them," Dick decided.

Meanwhile, Lije had been riding Whitey up-creek, stopping at every cabin on the way to ask, "Where's Lona at?" and wildly calling "Lona! Lona!" to the wooded ridges. No one had seen her since she passed that morning, and the woods only echoed back, "Ona! Ona!" Lije loved Lona in the dumb, dog-like way he loved the whole family on Wildcat Ridge, and, although she had been cured of her lameness, he still thought of her as a cripple who must be looked after. The news that she had not been to school and the mysterious note Rachel had given him struck terror to his heart. He must find her. He must hunt till he did.

As the dusk deepened, panic seized him. He would get back to Sairy Ann and Dick. They would know what to do. "Git along thar!" he shouted to Whitey every half minute. The old mule responded to the best of her ability, in spite of her stiff legs. She had been through many dangers and many hard places with her master and mistress, and she had never failed yet to do all she could in an hour of need.

"Where's Lona at?"

Sairy Ann and Dick rushed out to meet Lije as he rode up the path. "N-n-nobody knows where—where Lona's at, noways," he stammered in terror-stricken tones, so excited he forgot to deliver the note. At the sight of the envelope, Sairy snatched it from his hand, opened it, and read aloud:

Dear Aunt Sairy and Unkle Dick:
I've gone away to git me a job. Don't try to find me. I'm not a-comin' back, 'cept to visit. I love you, but I can't go to school no more. I shan't ever be smart like you.
Goodbye,
Lona

By the time she had finished, Sairy was almost in tears. "Oh, Dick! We've got to find her. Something dreadful may happen to her."

"Lije," said the doctor, "take the saddle off Whitey and put it on Twinkle." Twinkle was the new saddle horse that shared the stable with the white mule. She was a present from a former patient of Dick's down in the level country and was said to have ancestors of Kentucky Derby fame. She liked nothing better than a hurry call. Down the creek she went with Dick on her back, striking sparks from the stony road with her lightning-like hooves.

"Someone must be awful sick," said Grandma Slone as she peered out from the door of her one-room cabin at the foot of the Ridge. "Hope it ain't Sophy's boy, Mark; he wasn't so pert yesterday."

Sairy Ann gave Gail a bowl of bread and milk and tucked her into bed, thinking all the while of Lona. "I don't guess I love Gail much more than I do Lona," she said to herself as she kissed the baby's soft cheek and smiled into the blue eyes that were almost exact duplicates of her own. Lona was more like a little sister entrusted to her care than a daughter or a niece, for Sairy was only eleven years older than she.

She looked back over more than two years to that rainy night when she and Dick had found the child alone with her dying father in a miserable little cabin in the woods. Sairy shivered at the very thought of that damp, chilly place with the rain leaking through the roof. What a shadow of a real girl Lona was that night—little and thin and crippled and scared.

How pathetic she had been those first weeks after they had brought her home to live with them, limping about after them, afraid they might suddenly desert her. Then, the operation on her leg! Dick always said that she was the bravest patient he had ever had, and he meant it.

Sairy and he had seen the white, solemn wisp of a girl turn into this laughing, sparkling-eyed creature, who danced about as though she had just discovered that living was fun and she did not want to miss a minute of it. And she had grown beautiful. "Oh, Lona," said Sairy Ann out loud, "you must not get discouraged now, after all the way you have come."

A step sounded on the porch. Could it be Lona? Sairy could hardly conceal her disappointment when Grandma Slone shuffled in. "Anybody dyin'?" asked the old lady abruptly. "I jest see the doctor ridin' by like Satan was after him."

"No, Granny. Dick has just gone on an errand, and Twinkle is full of pep."

"That's strange," said Granny skeptically, "after she'd done gone clear up to Joe Slone's and back this mornin'." She picked out the most comfortable chair, adjusted the folds of her rusty black skirt, took out her pipe, thrust it between her toothless gums, and began to smoke. If there were any news, it was worth waiting for. But Sairy Ann talked only about the weather. Grandma finished her pipe and went off down the ridge path disappointed.

Chapter 3

Remember Amos

The lights in the cabins along the creek were all out by the time Dick came back. "Lona's at Blairstown most likely," he announced. "Several people saw her riding down Bull Creek with Bije this morning." Sairy looked somewhat relieved. Perhaps the old mail carrier would look after Lona.

"I'll start early after breakfast tomorrow and meet Bije on his up-trip and find out where she is," Dick planned out loud. "Then, if she is in Blairstown, I'll go down and see what my powers of persuasion can do."

Next morning after breakfast, Dick and Twinkle were off. "Thar he goes agin," muttered Granny Slone in an injured tone to her tame rooster. "Sairy Ann's keepin' somethin' from me. Somebody's punishin' bad, or he wouldn't be racin' up and down the creek night and mornin' that-a-way."

Twinkle was of the same opinion as Granny that someone was "punishin' bad" and had sent for the doctor in a hurry. She could tell from the way her master sat in the saddle that he was anxious to get somewhere. Down Hollybush Creek they sped, splashing through the Bull Creek ford to Slone's Creek. At the headwaters of Big Creek, Dick saw Bije's mules appearing around a bend in the road. The wagon followed, and on the seat sat Bije with a small, red-capped figure beside him.

"Whoa, Twinkle!" said Dick.

"What's he stopping here for?" Twinkle wondered, stamping impatiently.

"It's Uncle Dick!" In Lona's voice was great joy. Less than a minute was necessary for her to jump out of the wagon and climb up behind Dick on Twinkle's back.

"Was you coming to git me?" she asked.

"No, I was just coming to see you."

They rode in silence.

"I changed my mind," said Lona finally. "I decided this morning in bed that instead of being plucky, like I thought I was yesterday, I was jest running away from things."

"I rather hoped you'd see it that way sooner or later," said Dick quietly.

"I reckon if Amos could stand it, I kin."

"Amos?"

Lona told the story of Amos. "Somehow I couldn't fergit about him. I even dreamed about him last night."

They approached the Hollybush schoolhouse. From within came the sound of singing.

"You won't be very late," said Dick encouragingly.

Lona had a queer feeling at the pit of her stomach.

"I didn't aim to go back this morning."

"Longer you wait, the harder it will be," Dick advised, reining in Twinkle at the path.

For an instant, Lona hesitated. Then, with her nose in the air and her mouth set in a tight line, she went up the hill to the schoolhouse door.

"Came back, didn't you?" asked Rachel teasingly at recess.

Lona drew her aside. "If you dare break your promise and tell anybody about my running away, I'll die."

"Of course, I shan't break my promise, nohow," said Rachel, trying to act as though she had never intended to do such a thing.

"Remember Amos," said Lona firmly to herself when Miss Reed asked her to go to the map on the blackboard and bound the United States. "Remember Amos," she reminded herself when little Lilla Reynolds laughed out loud at a mistake she made in spelling class. Those two words became her slogan. They were to steady her in many an hour of need. Something Sairy Ann said that night helped, too.

"I knew that a girl who had been as brave as you have been would never run away from anything hard." That was all she ever said about the incident.

Chapter 4

The Box in the Attic

It was Saturday. Clouds hung low over Wildcat Ridge. A steady drizzle fell on the young corn. Lona looked out the window, disconsolately watching the tiny streams forcing their way through the thin soil and rushing pell-mell down to Hollybush Creek. As usual on a rainy Saturday, she was as restless as a caged squirrel. For many years, she had been sick and crippled. Now that she had two perfectly good legs, she liked to be using them.

"Oh, Lona, can't you find something to do besides watch the weather?" asked Sairy Ann when her patience with Lona's fidgets was exhausted. "You've been to the door at least ten times in the last half hour. Come on, you can help me clean the attic and pack away winter clothes. It's just the day for that job."

Lona sprang into action, pulling down the ladder stairway and climbing into the loft after Sairy as quickly as Whitenose could climb a tree. Up here was another world—peaceful and a little mysterious, especially at the dimly lighted end beneath the slope of the roof. The rain was pleasant music, pat-pattering overhead. Imprisoned flies buzzed sleepily. A mouse tiptoed out to investigate the unusual disturbance and scampered quickly back under the eaves at their approach. There was a delicious smell of camphor, cedarwood, and herbs mingled.

The front of the attic was Lije's sleeping quarters—a place of neatness and order—for the boy loved this room of his own after years of a somewhat badgered life in a one-room cabin. The dim end was full of a jumbled collection. The light of a lantern revealed boxes, trunks, bags, an old saddle, dried mint and sage, a few dry ears of corn, and some black walnuts left over from last year's gathering. Sairy Ann was amazed at the number of odds and ends that had accumulated in the short time she and Dick had lived here. But Lona was delighted. She nosed and poked about like a dog suddenly let loose in a yard full of smelly, long-buried bones. "What's this?" and "What's this?" and "Kin I have this?" she asked, till Sairy Ann declared she was more bother than help and begged her to stop asking questions.

Lona continued her explorations in silence. A small, rusty tin box with a tightly shut lid aroused her curiosity. The cover refused to yield to her prying fingers. She shook it, and rattlings and rustlings sounded within. She carried the box down to the kitchen and hacked and prodded it with a heavy-bladed knife. Finally, the rusty lid gave and opened to reveal a disappointingly uninteresting collection of articles.

On top was a ball of moth-eaten yarn with rusty knitting needles thrust through it and a half-knitted mitten attached. Beneath was a fine linen handkerchief, yellowed by time. Then Lona's inquisitive fingers brought out an old gold brooch, a little like one Grandma Gayheart wore, which in turn belonged to her mother. A crocheted baby's jacket was the next discovery, the white wool as yellow as the old handkerchief.

Who had left these small treasures so carefully stored away? Lona wondered. They had evidently lain there in the box for years. She pulled out the baby jacket, unfolding the small sleeves. They were edged with a peculiar, deep shade of blue. Where had she seen that jacket before? Not on Baby Gail. Not on any Hollybush baby. All at once she remembered. She had seen that jacket in her own mother's hands! Five or six years ago—it must have been as long as that—when the baby was coming, the baby that had lived only a week. So these were her mother's things. She poked a finger into each corner of the box, to make sure she had found everything. What was this? A time-blackened silver thimble.

Lona held the thimble, the brooch, and the handkerchief in her hand and unconsciously drew comfort from them. They were relics of those happier days she could not remember. She had heard her mother sigh for those days before her father had tried in vain to better himself by wandering from mill village to mill village, then to the coal mines, and finally resorting to woodcutting. She poked a finger into the last corner. There was nothing there but a small piece of yellowed paper with some indistinct marks on it and a few words of writing so faded Lona could not read it.

"What a help you turned out to be!" laughed Sairy Ann when she came downstairs. Lona sat with the contents of the tin box in her lap, looking dreamily into space.

"Aunt Sairy, what you s'pose I found up there in a box?"

"You could find almost anything, I should think. Of all the junk!"

Lona pointed to the things in her lap. "They're my own mother's. How did they git up there?"

Sairy Ann looked bewildered for a moment, then she remembered. "Why, that's a little box we found in the cabin after your pappy died. We brought it home along with you. Dick and I must have forgotten all about it—there were so many things to think about that day. Dick had to fix up a place in the barn for your cow, and I had to find a place for you to sleep and some things for you to wear and a bed for Whitenose.

Do you remember how you wouldn't go to sleep that night till I promised that the kitten could sleep right beside your bed?"

At the mention of her name, Whitenose, now a sleek, dignified cat and a great-grandmother, cocked one ear and half-opened one golden eye as she dozed on the rug. Lona bent down to smooth her gray velvet coat and put a caressing finger on the snowy tip of her nose. Whitenose purred appreciatively for a moment, then, convinced that no dinner was immediately forthcoming, continued her nap. Lona sat down on the arm of Sairy Ann's chair and gave her a breathtaking hug and a kiss. How could she ever love Sairy enough for all that she had done for her when she had been left alone in the world except for a mangy kitten and a bony old cow?

"I'm sorry about that box," said Sairy, returning Lona's hug and kiss. "I suppose it got carried up to the attic along with other things by mistake. Is there anything of much value in it?"

"They're valuable to me." Lona picked up the scrap of paper and looked at it again. "What you reckon this says?"

Sairy glanced at it and shook her head. "I can't make out; it's so faint."

Lona went close to the window and studied the faded marks and the few words in the corner. "F-o-r-t-y, forty, n-i-n-e, nine." Slowly, letter by letter and word by word, she spelled out "Forty-nine Snowballs."

"L-o-n-a A-l—," she began on the second line, then broke off. "Oh, Aunt Sairy! Aunt Sairy! It's my own name on this here paper—'Lona Allen.' Lookit."

"Why, it sure is your name. There must have been another Lona Allen a long time ago. Perhaps you were named for her."

Then Lona remembered something. "She was my pappy's aunt," she said, looking at the yellowed paper with awe. "I recollect Pappy telling me once that I was named fer her. Wonder what it means by 'Forty-nine Snowballs,' and what those crosses, or whatever they are, stand fer."

"Strange that it was kept all these years," said Sairy, and turned her attention to Gail, who always knew when it was dinnertime.

By the time dinner was cooked and eaten, Sairy Ann had forgotten all about the faded old paper. But Lona had not. The more she studied it, the more mysterious and exciting it seemed. She tried hard to decipher the faint marks. There were groups of crosses and almost obliterated lines. Did they mean something?

She remembered a story she had read in an old magazine. It was about a strange old miser who lived by himself. Everybody thought he was rich, but no one knew where he kept his money. When he died, his sisters and his nephews searched the place for hidden wealth, but there was none. In his desk, they found something that looked like a chart of some sort. It meant nothing to them, and they would have thrown it away if the youngest nephew had not saved it. The boy pored over the paper for days and even put it under a microscope. Finally, he decided that this chart was the clue to the hiding place of the money. After weeks of studying the paper and hunting, he found the old miser's wealth hidden within a hollow tree in the woods.

"What if this paper should prove to be a clue to some hidden treasure my great-aunt left?" thought Lona. When she mentioned the matter to Dick that evening and showed him the paper, he laughed at her. "Things like that happen in stories; they don't happen in real life," he said. "Haven't you found that out yet?"

Lona tucked the paper back in a corner of the rusty box and put the box in her chest of drawers. Anyway, she was going to keep that old paper.

Chapter 5

Two Cakes for One Party

One morning after breakfast, about a month later, Dick beckoned stealthily to Lona as he started for his office in the clinic. "Sit down a minute. I've got something on my mind," he said in a tone that was almost a whisper. He shut the door tight and began to explain his mysterious behavior.

"Saturday is Sairy Ann's birthday. What do you say we have a play-party?"

Nothing could have suited Lona better. Her smile was answer enough to the question.

"Can you manage the birthday cake? Mammy Hall will let you make it up there, and I will supply the candles."

Lona expanded with pride at the thought of being responsible for so important a matter.

"Now for guests," went on Dick. "Pappy and Mammy Hall, and Preacher Johnny, and Grandma Slone, of course." (They were always included in any good times on the ridge.) "Then I thought we might ask the mothers and fathers who are bringing their babies to the baby clinic. And Miss Barnes, if she can get away." (Miss Barnes was almost Sairy Ann's patron saint. As principal of the Slone's Creek School and Community Center, she had encouraged her to go to high school and then to go down to the level country and train to be a nurse.)

"How about Dan and Nancy? He could fetch his fiddle and play and sing." Dan Hall, Sairy's brother, was a famous fiddler on the creek.

"Fine idea, Lona. That's probably all we'd better ask. I don't want you to have to bake the cake in a washtub."

"Reckon I'll have to bake it in a dishpan." Lona's eyes sparkled in anticipation of the occasion. Suddenly she grew grave. "I wish that I had a birthday. I reckon I'm the only girl on Hollybush, reckon I'm the only girl in the world, that doesn't know when her birthday is. It makes me feel so strange."

Dick looked sympathetic. "Wish I could give you one." It was true that Lona was birthday-less. That is, nobody knew which day in the year she could claim. Birthdays had been left uncelebrated in the miserable cabin where Sairy Ann and Dick had found her, and there was no record left of her birth. She only knew that she would be fourteen sometime during the spring.

After Lona had gone out, Dick sat at his desk for a time, looking thoughtful. On his way up-creek to visit a patient, he reined in Twinkle at his mother-in-law's gate. "I suppose Lona told you about the play-party for Sairy Ann on the fifteenth?" he asked.

Mammy Hall nodded.

"We'll need two cakes instead of one."

"Two cakes? What you aimin' to do with two?" asked Mammy.

"One for Sairy and one for Lona. I've made up my mind that Lona's going to have a birthday. She knows she was born in the spring. So I've decided to call the sixteenth her birthday and celebrate it at the same time as Sairy Ann's. I'll get pink candles for Lona and yellow ones for Sairy."

Thus it came about that two birthday cakes were baked in Mammy's oven. The one Lona made under Mammy's supervision. The other Lona knew nothing about.

"Aunt Sairy will be the most surprised she's ever been," exulted Lona as she frosted the big cake. "She'll be surprised to have frosting on her cake, and she'll be a heap surprised to see Miss Barnes and Dan there. Dan's a-going to fetch his fiddle and sing song-ballads and play fer a Virginia Reel. Won't it be fun, Mammy Hall, to see Sairy Ann's face when they all begins to come!"

***

On the night of the party, Sairy Ann's surprise was as nothing compared to that of Lona's. Her eyes widened when Rachel Hall and Jimmy Hayes arrived. She hadn't expected to see them, nor old Grandma Gayheart's youngest grandson, Peter. "I wonder if they came without an invitation," she thought. Her face was practically all eyes when the second cake, containing fourteen candles, was brought in and set down in front of her.

"'Tain't my birthday—"

"Ladies and gentlemen," began Dick, before Lona could say more. "We are killing two birds with one stone and celebrating two birthdays with one party—but not with one cake," he added, looking first at Sairy's cake and then at Lona's. "Today is the birthday of Sairy Ann Hall Lawrence, and tomorrow is the birthday of Lona Allen."

"But—but, Uncle Dick," began Lona.

"This is no time for 'buts.' Let's have the candle-blowing." Dick gave her a look as he spoke that seemed to say, "Play the game; I'll explain later."

She and Sairy blew at the same time. All eyes turned toward Lona's cake, where four candles remained burning.

"You ain't a-goin' to git married till you're eighteen," said Grandma Slone with disappointment in her voice. "I was married when I was fifteen."

At this point, a wail rose from Baby Gail. "Light! Light!"

she demanded, for she had never seen such beautiful lights as those birthday candles before and could not see why they were all blown out. But her smiles came back when a piece of cake was placed in her hands, and she proceeded to smear the lower half of her face with frosting.

The table was cleared, and Dan produced his fiddle. Pounding a heavy boot toe on the floor to keep time, he began to sing:

> *"'Twas in the merry month of May,*
> *With the green leaves bustin' all around—"*

One by one, other voices joined his until all the roomful of people were tapping their feet and raising their voices in the sweetly plaintive strains of the old song-ballad.

Even Gail tried to sing the chorus. So did Lizzie Gayheart's year-old baby, after her fashion, and Mattie Boleyn's two-year-old son. Strange discords were produced, but nobody minded.

"Everybody on their feet for a Virginia Reel," shouted Dan Hall, breaking into—

> *"Chicken crowing on Sourwood Mountain,*
> *Hey ho, diddle dum dee-ay."*

"Choose your partners."

> *"My true love's a blue-eyed daisy,*
> *Hey ho, diddle dum dee-ay."*

"My true love's a black-eyed Susan," sang Peter Gayheart as he lined up opposite Lona, to her amazement, and bowed with mock formality. She stood in awe of this handsome, eighteen-year-old boy who was a senior in the Slone's Creek High School.

"Swing your partners," called Dan and began to sing—

"Chicken crowing on Sourwood Mountain,
Hey ho diddle dum dee-ay."

> *"Big dog bark and little one bite you,*
> *Hey ho diddle dum dee-ay.*
> *Big gal'll court and little one'll slight you,*
> *Hey ho diddle dum dee-ay."*

"Hope that's not true about little girls," said Peter, looking down at Lona's black head that did not nearly reach to his shoulder. Lona grinned.

"Grand right and left," ordered Dan, before she had time to answer. All the rest of the evening, she was conscious that her partner in the reel was watching her.

"Tell us some stories, Pappy," begged Sairy Ann when the reel was ended. "Tell the one about Pete, the one-eyed mule."

"Wal," began Pappy, "Pete was a mule that was the property of old Uncle Jim Pease. Now Uncle Jim, he was deaf in both his ears, and the mule, it was blind in one eye. Wal, one day when Uncle Jim was a-ridin' Pete up Coon Holler …"

Pappy kept his listeners in a broad grin for twenty minutes with his famous mule story. Then there was a call for "The Wedding on Breakneck Mountain." By the time the second story was ended, the fire on the hearth had burned low.

Soon the play-party broke up. Late parties are unknown on Hollybush Creek, where there are always a goodly number of babies among the guests. They went down the ridge path, a little procession on foot and on muleback, their way lighted by gleams of lantern light.

The smile that had appeared on Lona's face at the announcement of her birthday had scarcely left it during the evening. It seemed to have grown there.

"What did you mean, Uncle Dick, by saying it was my birthday?" she asked.

Dick produced a long, legal-looking sheet of paper with a homemade seal affixed to it and handed it to Lona. It read:

Know all men by these presents that I, Richard Lawrence, being of sound mind, do hereby name and set aside the day May sixteenth as the birthday of Lona Allen. This day is to be regarded her natal day so long as she may live.

Signed and sealed this fifteenth day of May nineteen hundred and —.

Richard Lawrence, M.D.

Lona was as much impressed as though it were a court document. "Sounds like it was the truth, but how do you know that's the right day?"

"I don't, but there's no reason in the world why you can't pick out a day and call it yours. And I rather thought you'd like a day you could celebrate along with Sairy Ann. Is that satisfactory?"

"Oh, yes! It makes me feel like other girls. I reckon everybody at the party thought it really was my birthday, don't you?"

"Of course they did. Now, Sairy Ann, will you just sign your name as a witness?"

Lona put the make-believe document in the old tin box. "I shall keep it always," she said. And she did.

Chapter 6

The Wooden Cat

It was the day after the birthday party. Lona was out in the yard playing a rather one-sided game of ball with Gail. She was free to do nearly as she pleased now, for school was closed for the long vacation. Gail gave a wild toss, and the ball went careening down the steep slope. Lona raced after it. She had just given up hope of saving the ball from a bath in the creek when a tall figure rose in the path below her. It was Peter Gayheart. Making a dive for the runaway ball, he tossed it lightly to Lona.

"Howdy," said he with a grin.

"Howdy," said Lona, wondering whether he had come to see Sairy Ann, Dick, or her. She decided to find out. "Thar ain't nobody home but me and the baby," she announced. "Joe Slone's awful sick, and Aunt Sairy and Uncle Dick has gone up to his cabin."

Peter did not seem to be disturbed by this news. "I came for to see you," he said.

They walked up the path together and sat down on the porch. "It was a fine play-party last night," said Peter. "I didn't know it was going to be your birthday party when I came. Doctor Dick didn't tell me that."

Lona almost said that she hadn't known it was her birthday party, either. "I reckon I had as much fun as anybody," she said, smiling at the recollection of the happy surprise it had been for her.

There was an awkward silence. Peter got up, sat down again, got up, and walked up and down the porch; in fact, he acted as though there were something he wanted to say and he did not know how to start. All the while, he kept one hand in his coat pocket, where there seemed to be a bulky object. Lona wished she could think of something to say.

"I—I've got something here I made. Maybe you'd like it for a sort of a birthday present." He took his hand from his pocket and with it a small, irregular-shaped object wrapped in a brown paper. He held it out to her.

"This is the best birthday surprise of all," thought Lona, as she drew from its wrapping a small cat carved from wood.

"Oh-h-h-h! What a beautiful present! You made it yourself?" she asked, hardly able to believe that Peter or anyone else had created this graceful, lifelike cat out of a block of wood.

Peter nodded. "Does it look like Whitenose?"

"Point-blank. But I didn't know you ever heard of Whitenose."

"My memory's better than yourn. I saw Whitenose the first time I ever saw you."

"I don't recollect it, noways."

"I went to the doctor to get him to pull me a tooth. You were a-limping around in the yard with Whitenose in your arms. That was before the doctor cured you. I asked you if it was your kitten, and you said yes. Then I asked you her name, and I can see you now, the way you looked up at me solemnly and said, 'Whitenose, she's all the family I've got now.'"

"I reckon I was mighty solemn those days."

"But you're not now. I think you'd be a lot of fun to know well."

They both smiled, and there was no more shyness between them. Peter began to talk about his plans. In another year, he would be through high school. Then he was going down to the level country to a school where they taught people to draw and model. After that, he was coming back to Hollybush to have a little workshop of his own and make things to sell—things carved from wood and cut out of iron, and dishes he would make of clay.

"I'm practicing now on making dishes," he said.

"What do you want to go to school in the level country fer, when you kin make a cat like that already?"

Peter laughed. "That cat is just a beginning. I want to learn to do much better."

"Don't see how nobody could," Lona persisted.

After Peter had gone, Lona sat for a long time looking at the wooden cat in her hand, admiring the delicate carving of the ears and toes, the smoothness of the wood, and the grain so beautifully brought out by Peter's polishing.

"It's beautiful. Maybe," she mused, "he will be a great sculpterer someday and make statues like those in the pictures over at the Slone's Creek School." She went to the chest of drawers in her room, took out the old tin box and tucked the cat into a corner. Somehow she felt like keeping the gift a secret between Peter and herself.

"I wish," said Lona that night as the family sat at the supper table, "that I could make something fine-pretty."

"What do you want to make?" asked Sairy Ann.

"I don't know what—jest something so beautiful that everybody would like to look at it—a picture, maybe."

"Well, keep on wishing hard, and maybe you will," said Sairy, encouragingly.

Chapter 7

Mammy Airs Her Kivers

Mammy Hall gave a final pat to a pale yellow mold of freshly churned butter, then carried it to the cool springhouse. On her way back, she stopped, shaded her eyes with a thin brown hand, and looked up at the young corn that grew almost to the top of the steep ridge. "I reckon that hoein' can wait another day," she said to herself; "my poor old back needs a rest." With an "Ah-h-h" of relief, she settled down in a hickory split-bottomed chair on the porch.

A soft smile of anticipation suddenly lighted her wrinkled face. "I'll air my kivers," she decided. Forgetful of her "poor back," she dragged a large wooden chest out on the porch. One by one she lifted up the homespun bed coverlets. Her touch was the lingering caress of a miser fingering hoarded gold. She did not hear Lona's step on the porch. It would have taken a far heavier tread to disturb that happy reverie.

Lona spent much of her time here in the cabin that had been Sairy Ann's home before she married Dick. Sometimes she played with Rachel, the "least" child of the family, but almost as often she talked with Mammy. There was great love and understanding between this wise, middle-aged woman and the orphaned girl who had been taken into her daughter's home. Mammy's big heart had opened wide to receive Lona the first moment she had seen her limping forlornly about the house on the ridge. And the girl had found a permanent place in that heart.

"Why, Mammy Hall," exclaimed Lona, "you look like you was a hundred miles away."

"Oh, child, I was pretty near a hundred years away. Look at that now." She pointed to the corner of the ancient blue-and-white coverlet that lay across her lap. Woven into the creamy background was—

ABIGAIL HUGHES
1835

"My grandma wove it 'fore she was married. She come nigh to losin' it once—in the war between the States. The soldiers come and took all her victuals and blankets and things. When they grabbed this here kiver, she stood right up to them, and she said, 'I wove that when I was a gal. It took two years to git me enough wool to spin fer it, from Pappy's sheep. I was two years a-weavin' it fer my marriage chest. It's kept me and my man warm fer nigh thirty years. Are ye a-goin' to take an old woman's bed kiver from her and drag it through the mud?' And the general, or whatever he was, said to the soldiers, 'Put it back,' and they done put it back on the bed."

"Oh, Mammy, ain't it beautiful," said Lona, holding up one corner. "What do you call that pattern?"

"'Double Chariot Wheels.' This here is 'Pine-bloom,'" she said, lifting a brown-and-white coverlet from the chest. "And this"—she pulled out another treasure—"I done the year before Sairy Ann was born. It's called 'Governor's Garden.'" Woven in dull reds and soft blue, it looked not a little like a formal garden in which a governor might be proud to promenade.

Together they unfolded the coverlets, hung them on the clothesline, and brushed them. When they were all flapping in the breeze, Lona exclaimed with delight, "They're like flower beds hung up instead of on the ground."

While they worked, Mammy described how the old covers were made—the spinning of the wool, the different plants and barks that were used in making the dyes for the wool, the setting up of the loom.

"Seems such a little time ago Aunt Betsy and I was dyein' the wool for that 'Governor's Garden' kiver," said Mammy.

"You mean Aunt Betsy the herb-woman?" asked Lona, surprised. "I didn't know she could do anything but make bitter medicines."

Mammy nodded. "Thar ain't nobody in this county knows so much about makin' dyes. They used to send for her from way down Big Creek way and from over yonways." She pointed vaguely to the east.

Lona felt a new respect for the queer, witch-like old woman who was always brewing herbs in her great iron pot.

Seated on the porch again, both fell to musing. The thoughts of the one were of the past; the other's were of the future.

"Mammy Hall," said Lona, so suddenly that Mammy jumped. "Do you reckon I could learn to weave me a kiver?"

"What's that you say?" asked Mammy, distrusting her ears.

Lona repeated her question.

"Of course you could learn, if you'd have patience. I was weavin' when I was your age."

"I reckon I'd feel like I'd painted me a fine-pretty picture, if I could make one," said Lona.

"You'd have to git ye a loom," said Mammy.

Lona had not thought of that. "Couldn't Preacher Johnny make me one?" Preacher Johnny made furniture and did odd carpentry jobs on weekdays and preached at the schoolhouse on Sundays.

Mammy Hall pondered for a moment. "I wonder if my old loom could be fixed up. It's down behind the washhouse, and the chickens have been a-roostin' on it fer years."

Lona was off the porch and on her way to the washhouse before the last sentence was finished. The old loom was, as Mammy put it, "a sorry sight." Some of the treadles were broken, and other important parts were missing. It was crusted all over with dirt. Mammy shook her head doubtfully, but Lona was undismayed. "First, we'll give it a good washing," she announced cheerfully and ran to fetch a bucket of water.

Rachel, who had returned from a trip to the store, looked on scornfully. "What you aim to do with that dirty old loom?" she asked.

"I aims to weave a beautiful bed kiver," said Lona. "But promise you won't tell Sairy Ann. I want to surprise her."

"I won't tell," agreed Rachel.

But Lona distrusted her playmate's memory. "Rachel," she said, "if you keeps that promise, you kin wear my red beads for a whole week."

A smile of utter delight spread over Rachel's face. "Does you mean it?" she asked, hardly believing she had heard aright. The red beads were Lona's most prized possession, partly because Sairy Ann had given them to her and partly because she had never had beads or jewelry of any kind before.

"I shan't open my lips about the kiver," promised Rachel, and this time Lona knew she meant it.

Back and forth, back and forth went Lona from the spring to the loom and from the loom to the spring. Determinedly, she battled with the accumulated dirt of years. Her arms and back ached, but she paid no attention to their complaints. "Better stop and eat your dinner, child," Mammy advised her. Lona was not interested in dinner. She kept on scrubbing till the wood of the ancient loom was as white as Mammy Hall's kitchen table. Then she took a plate of fried ham and spoon bread to her favorite spot—the springhouse—and ate from the sunny milk-pan shelf outside the door. For dessert, she picked the sweet wild strawberries that grew by the wall.

"I don't know," she said to herself dreamily as she looked at the airing coverlets, "whether I'd rather make me a 'King's Flower,' a 'Sun, Moon, and Stars' or a 'Double Chariot Wheels'; anyway, I'll weave my name into the corner, jest like Abigail Hughes did."

Preacher Johnny, when called in that afternoon, looked at the loom with the grave face of a doctor studying a patient in a critical condition. He pulled thoughtfully at his long gray beard and pronounced it "in mighty bad shape." The loom, rescued from the weather and the chickens, stood now in the old log cabin, once called the "weaving cabin," where two generations of women had spun and woven and quilted.

"You reckon, Miz Hall, you're goin' to do some weavin' right now in the middle o' hoein' time?" he asked skeptically.

"I might." Mammy, too, had been sworn to secrecy about Lona's plans.

"Wal, I'm fixin' a desk fer the doctor now. May be a week, may be more, 'fore I'm done."

"Uncle Dick ain't in no hurry fer that desk," interrupted Lona. "I know he'd want you to fix Mammy Hall's loom first."

The old man meditated. "Tomorrow's the Sabbath. Monday I has to git my mule shod and hoe corn. Tuesday I'm a-preachin' over on Bull Creek to the funeral meetin'. I reckon I could work over here on Wednesday, the Lord willin'."

It was settled that the preacher should come on Wednesday, but it seemed to Lona a long time to wait. He started down the path, humming his favorite hymn, "I'm a-goin' to shine like a star in the mornin'." Then he stopped and retraced his steps. "I recollect now it's the dark o' the moon on Wednesday," he announced. "That's a bad time to begin a piece o' work."

Mammy looked troubled, but Lona brushed aside the difficulty. "This ain't a new piece o' work. This is jest fixin' over an old piece."

Again the preacher agreed to come on Wednesday. "But, mark you," he warned, "I don't guarantee noways the loom won't break down on you. The dark o' the moon is a bad time, a bad time."

Chapter 8

Lona's House

"I'm going to call it my house," said Lona, as she explored Mammy Hall's cobwebby old weaving cabin. In the center, filling most of the floor space, stood the old loom, conspicuously mended with bright new wood. In one corner was a spinning wheel. In another, a reel held out empty pegs, as though waiting for Mammy to come and "put up her warp."

"The place is yourn," said Mammy.

Once more Lona brought out broom and scrubbing pail. The spiders and the wasps that had occupied the place for years moved out in a state of indignation. By noon, the cabin must have felt that time had gone backward. Its walls and floor were clean and free from cobwebs. A fire glowed again on the soot-blackened hearth, and smoke rose cheerfully from the century-old chimney. Two chairs and two rag rugs from the house gave the place a homelike look. At the reel stood Mammy and Lona, filling the pegs with the threads of white warp they unwound from a great spool.

Rachel looked on from the door. "When you coming out to play, Lona?" she asked every few minutes. Lona decided to discourage that question once and for all. "I'm a-going to stay right in this cabin today, tomorrow, the next day, the day after that—maybe the whole vacation," she announced. Rachel looked at Lona, feeling sure her playmate had suddenly lost her senses, and wandered away to find Jimmy Hayes.

"I reckon that's enough fer a rug," said Mammy, ceasing her rhythmic movements at the reel and beginning to form the long loops of warp into a braid. "Now you run home to your dinner, and this afternoon we'll thread up."

Lona looked amazed. "A rug? Don't look like nowhere near enough fer a kiver to me. That's what I aims to make."

"You ain't ready to make no kiver yet awhile," Mammy told her. "I'm goin' to start ye in on a rag rug while yer learnin.'" Thus, suddenly, was Lona awakened to the size of the task she was undertaking.

"Where have you been all the morning?" Sairy Ann inquired when Lona presented herself a little late for dinner. On vacation days, she was usually Sairy's right-hand man about the house.

If weaving a coverlet was going to take a long time, some explanation of her unwonted absences from home would have to be made, the girl had decided. "Up to Mammy Hall's. She says I can have the old weaving cabin to use like it was mine. She's a-going to learn me to weave a rag rug. I reckon I'll be up there most all the time fer a spell, 'cepten when you needs me."

Sairy Ann smiled and made up her mind to call Lona away from her weaving as little as possible. She had not seen such a look of enthusiasm on the girl's face for months.

Dick became interested. "If you can weave a good-looking rug, I'll buy it off you for the clinic."

Lona put down her knife and fork. It had never occurred to her that she would find a market for her weaving. "Does you mean it, Uncle Dick? Honest?"

"Honest," he assured her. "Here, hold on a minute. That rug can wait till you've had your dinner."

Lona came back and sat down at the table. In her excitement, she had started for the cabin, completely forgetting that she had not finished her dinner.

"Clackety-clack! Clackety-clack!" sounded from the weaving cabin all that afternoon. Within sat Lona at the loom, threading a rag-wound shuttle through the warp. As she worked, she sang softly the last lines of an old hymn she had often heard Mammy sing:

> *"With perfect delight*
> *By day and by night*
> *This wonderful song I'll sing."*

The song fitted her mood. Nothing she had ever done before had given her such perfect delight. Even the weaving of a rag rug—a comedown from her plan to start at once on a coverlet—was fun. Fun! Why, it was a miracle to see this firm, many-colored cloth grow out of rags and string.

"You took to weavin' quickest of anyone I ever knowed," was Mammy's surprised comment.

"Your rug is going to save my prescribing lots of medicines, Lona. One good look at those bright colors ought to be equal to a bottle of tonic."

Dick Lawrence stood in the clinic and looked at the new rug spread in front of his desk. It represented two solid weeks of hard work for Lona, but what happy weeks they had been!

She beamed proudly. "Maybe I'll make another; Mammy Hall has more rags." She was off for the weaving cabin.

Sairy Ann smiled at her husband when he told her that Lona was making another rug. "If this enthusiasm continues, she'll have the clinic and the whole house carpeted."

However, Lona had no intention of making more rugs. Her remark was only a smokescreen to conceal more important activities. She was on her way now to start weaving a coverlet under Mammy's direction.

When she reached the cabin, Mammy Hall was standing in the doorway, looking as though "Bad News" were her name.

"Child, I can't find my drafts. I thought I could put my hand right on them. I always kept them in one place—in that little holler back of the chimney. But they ain't there."

"What's a draft?" asked Lona as soon as Mammy gave her a chance to open her mouth.

"Jest a little piece o' paper that shows how to weave the pattern. You can't do no weavin' withouten that."

"Oh, Mammy Hall, think hard. We've got to find one." Lona's tone was desperate. She was going to weave one of those old coverlets, and nothing should stop her. She could see it finished in dull rose, soft gray, and tan, like a huge picture. Next week Aunt Betsy was to help her make the dyes for the long-stored wool Mammy had turned over to her. She began feverishly hunting—in the cupboard, in the old chest full of the wool that waited to be woven, behind the reel.

"I don't reckon thar's any bit o' use lookin'," said Mammy. "I never put them nowhere else 'cepten that one place. Might be the rats et them, or might be somebody borried them and never brung them back."

The old woman and the girl looked at each other with the despairing gaze of those who have had rich treasures and have lost them. But Lona wouldn't give up. "I'm a-going to hunt till I kin find a draft or somebody that kin draw me one."

Chapter 9

The Hunt That Ended at Home

Lona had always been a little afraid of Aunt Betsy, as everyone on Hollybush called her. She looked like an old witch, toothless, shriveled, with black eyes that seemed to penetrate one's flesh like X-rays. Witchlike she was this morning as she stirred up an herb medicine, black as her old black kettle. Lona knew that the old woman's tongue could be as bitter as her medicines, but the girl forgot her fears on her quest.

"Oh, child, I ain't made kivers fer twenty years or more, not since my right eye was poor. I didn't never have no drafts, 'cepten 'Sun, Moon, and Stars' and 'Pine Bloom,' and I must have burnt them up. What do you want o' them old drafts?"

Lona explained. "But please don't tell Aunt Sairy; it's to be a surprise."

"Surprise! Humph! It will be a surprise to me if you ever gits it done," mumbled Aunt Betsy pessimistically.

Lona's next call was on Aunt Sally. The result was much the same as at Aunt Betsy's, except for the sweet smile and the piece of cake this old lady gave her.

Lona tried not to show her impatience to get on with her search. But she could not help fidgeting while the old lady spent an hour telling of the wool she had carded and spun and woven and made into clothes when she was young.

By afternoon, all nearby possible possessors of weaving drafts had been canvassed, and Lona was riding Whitey up Coon Hollow to Grandma Gayheart's. Grandma was a hundred years old, according to her own reckoning. There were those who doubted it and said she could not possibly be so "pert" at that age. Certainly she was the oldest person for miles around and, in Lona's opinion, the nicest.

Peter Gayheart straightened out his six-foot frame that was curved over the sawhorse in the yard. He was spending the afternoon with his grandmother, working on her woodpile.

"Howdy, Lona," he called. "Did you come to see me?"

Lona looked pleasantly scornful.

"I have special business with your granny," she said.

Grandma, sitting on her porch shelling beans, took off her black sunbonnet and gingham apron at the sight of a visitor. "If it ain't Lona Allen," she exclaimed delightedly. "How's Sairy Ann? How's the doctor? Is he doctorin' many folks now? Is the baby growin'? Did Pappy Hall git better o' the grippe?" An avalanche of questions descended upon the girl. Not until the old lady had been supplied with all the news on Hollybush did Lona have a chance to state her errand.

"Weavin' drafts? Land sakes! I ain't had a shuttle in my hand since Dan was a baby. I give my wheel and my loom and all my drafts to my gal Sarah, when she got married. She was the weavingest woman in these parts, I reckon. But poor Sarah's dead now, and it's probable those things are all lost or burnt up."

Grandma forgot about weaving. Her faded eyes grew misty. "I didn't think Sarah would go 'fore I did," she said, wiping her spectacles, and was silent for a long time.

Lona sighed. "I sure wish I could find one of them drafts."

"Child, I plumb forgot you was here," said the old lady suddenly. "Now you go and fetch that tin bucket that's hangin' there in the well, and we'll have some buttermilk."

"I'll fetch it, Grandma," volunteered Peter from the doorstep, where he had been listening in on the conversation.

"Grandma, what does a weaving draft look like, anyhow?" asked Lona as she sipped the cool buttermilk.

"Jest a lot o' lines and crosses to show how the pattern goes—What's the matter, child?" asked the old lady, for Lona had jumped from her chair as if shot out of it.

"Did you ever hear of a kiver called 'Forty-nine Snowballs'?" She was so excited she could hardly wait for the answer.

"Why, y-yes, I reckon I have. If I remember right, Sarah made one, and it was a beauty. There's one called 'Nine Snowballs,' too. What's your hurry, child? Seems like you had only jest got here, and you ain't drunk all your buttermilk."

"I've got to go right home and look fer something." She was off the porch in one jump.

"I'll unhitch your mule," said Peter, hurrying after her. He untied Whitey, then picked Lona up as though she were a bit of nothing at all and set her on the white mule's back.

The first thing Lona did when she reached home was to go to the chest of drawers in her room and take from the rusty tin box the yellow slip of paper that bore her name. Tucking it into the front of her dress, she started for Mammy Hall's.

"I've got a draft fer my kiver," she proclaimed, doing a sort of dance of triumph around Mammy, who sat on the porch hulling wild strawberries. "And where you reckon I found it?"

"Did Grandma Gayheart give it to you?"

"No, you never could guess. It was in an old box in the attic, and it used to be my great-aunt's, and I was named fer her, and it's called, 'Forty-nine Snowballs.' Lookit." Lona stopped for breath and handed the precious piece of paper to Mammy.

"'Forty-nine Snowballs,'" repeated the old woman. "Yes, I've heard tell of that pattern." The network of wrinkles around her eyes deepened into creases as she squinted at the paper. She held it at arm's length. Then she laughed.

"Looks to me like a chicken done walked across that paper 'bout a hundred years ago. I can't make nothin' out of it."

Lona's face lengthened, and the lights in her eyes went out. "But there's lines and crosses on it," she persisted.

Mammy tried again. "Yes," she said, "it's a weavin' draft, no two ways 'bout that, but it's not clear enough to go by."

"Got a pencil?" asked Lona.

"There's one somewheres, if I kin find it." Mammy Hall searched the cabin and finally came back with a stub of a pencil. Lona spread the paper out on the rough porch floor, sat down on the step, and went to work tracing over the faint marks. Mammy finished hulling berries and began getting supper. The girl worked on, bowed low over the paper, frowning in her efforts to make out the crosses and lines that time had tried hard to blot out.

Finally, she got up and went into the kitchen. "Lookit," she said, putting the paper down right on top of the biscuit dough.

"Git that paper off my dough," ordered Mammy.

Lona picked it up and held it in front of Mammy's face. "Wal, wal, if you ain't got good eyes in your head! I couldn't make it out, noways."

Lona kissed first one of her thin, wrinkled cheeks and then the other. "Let's set up the loom right now, please," she begged.

"Lona Allen, have you gone plumb crazy? You run along home and let me git Pappy's supper and milk the cow."

Chapter 10

With Perfect Delight

Lona felt like an old witch woman as she dug up sassafras roots in the woods and pulled off long strips of bark from the maple trees on the ridge for making dyes for her wool.

"Maybe I'll look like Aunt Betsy pretty soon," she thought. Next day, she felt more like a witch than ever as she stood over the herb-woman's kettle, learning how to make the colors she wanted and how to set them so that they would never fade.

"When did you dig them sassafras roots?" asked Aunt Betsy. "Did you dig them in the full o' the moon like I told ye to?"

"Yes, Aunt Betsy," answered Lona, smiling.

"You kin smile, child, but it makes all the difference in the world. Once I used sassafras roots dug in the new moon, and I got the most awful bilious color you ever did see."

For most of two days, the girl's back was bent over the kettle, following the old woman's directions to the letter—brewing strange-smelling, strange-looking mixtures and boiling her wool in them. When the long strands of yarn were dry, she gathered them into her arms and looked at Aunt Betsy with awe in her eyes.

"They're jest the colors I wanted. Ain't that the prettiest pink you ever did see?" She held up a hank of old-rose colored

For most of two days, the girl's back was bent over the kettle.

yarn as she spoke. "It's the color the clouds are 'fore the sun comes up."

Aunt Betsy, Lona decided, was more like a magician than a witch, since she knew how to transform dirty-looking wool into a rainbow of beautiful colors.

"Why, look at your hands!" exclaimed Sairy Ann that night as Lona sat down to supper.

"I've been helping Aunt Betsy brew her herbs."

"If you've time to work for the neighbors, you might help me hoe the garden tomorrow," suggested Uncle Dick.

"All right," assented Lona faintly. Ordinarily, she would have considered hoeing with Uncle Dick fun. But not now, when Mammy had the loom all threaded up, her yarns were dyed, and she was ready to begin the "Forty-nine Snowballs."

On the morrow, Lona as a garden-hoer was a distinct failure. "Hi, there! You hoed up a bean plant then instead of a weed," called Dick.

"What?" asked Lona, bringing her thoughts back from the weaving cabin to the garden.

"What's the matter with you today, anyway?"

"I was thinking of something else," she explained.

After this performance had been repeated several times, Dick told Lona, to her great relief, that she was fired. She had not tried to bring this result about, but she simply couldn't keep her mind on mere weeds when the loom and the soft-hued yarns and the old weaving draft waited for her in the cabin.

There followed for Lona days of weaving and singing "with perfect delight." Beneath her shuttle the "Forty-nine Snowballs" pattern took form in the soft colors of the wool she had dyed. Yes, her great-aunt had left her a treasure, and she had found it with the help of the old yellow paper. Perhaps, thought Lona, that Lona Allen, whose name was on the paper, sat up there beyond the clouds somewhere, listening to the music of harps and looking down and smiling to see that her grandniece had found her legacy of beauty.

*"Good morning, good morning, good morning to thee,
Oh, where are you going, my pretty lady?"*

At the sound of a tenor voice singing the old song-ballad, Lona turned to see Peter Gayheart standing in the doorway of her cabin.

*"Oh, I am a-going to the banks of the sea,
To see the waters a-gliding, hear the nightingale sing."*

Lona finished the stanza. "As a matter of fact," she added, laughing, "I'm a-going to stay right here and weave, and it ain't 'good morning'; it's 'good afternoon.'"

Peter grinned. "Look at the little old-fashioned girl! What do you think you're doing with Mammy Hall's old loom?"

"Weaving me a kiver."

He leaned over and looked at the narrow strip of cloth across which Lona's hands moved rapidly, then gave a low whistle. "Why, it's one of those old bed kivers like Aunt Sarah used to make, and it's going to be a beauty, too." The joking tone had gone out of his voice. "I thought you were different from the other girls," he said admiringly. "I don't guess there's another girl on Hollybush Creek or in this county that would bother to learn to weave."

Lona laid down her shuttle and told him the story of her hunt for a draft and the old paper in the tin box.

"After that, you deserve to make your fortune weaving," said Peter. "Now I've got something to show you." He took a round package out of his pocket. It was a sugar bowl, shaped with his own hands out of clay and glazed a dull yellow. Instead of a round knob on the cover, a small black rooster stood looking as though he might crow any minute.

"Why, it's Granny Slone's tame rooster, point-blank," Lona exclaimed.

"That's what I aimed it to be. I'm making a pitcher and a teapot, and when they're done, Miss Barnes says she wants to buy them off me, and cups and saucers, too."

Lona looked at Peter's long-fingered, strong-fingered, brown hands with awe. "You sure kin do wonderful things with your hands, Peter."

He laughed and looked at her hand that held the shuttle ready to slip it through the warp. "So can you."

"How did you make it shiny like that? And did you paint the colors on?"

He explained how the glaze was put on and how the colors came out after the dish was baked and described the firing of his dishes in Abe Hall's kiln on Big Creek. He was silent for a moment, deep in thought.

"Lona," he said, "somebody has got to do something on this creek besides scratch these poor old hills and plant corn on them, or everybody's bound to starve sooner or later. I believe you and I can help Hollybush someday. We can show people how to earn money by doing things they have forgotten how to do. Folks from all over the country will hear about Hollybush Creek and the weaving and woodcarving and pottery we do here. It's been done in other places, and we can do it. And we'll make our things different so that everyone will say, 'That's from Hollybush Creek; it's different.'"

Peter looked across the creek to the top of Wildcat Ridge, where the sunset clouds were golden. His fine gray eyes kindled at what he saw, but he was not seeing the sunset. He was looking into the future. Lona followed his glance and his thoughts. Her eyes, too, lighted with a vision of what they might do in the years out there ahead, years that looked as golden as the clouds to these young people.

Lona of Hollybush Creek

"Well," said Peter reluctantly, "I reckon I'll have to be going along home."

Lona watched him go down the path toward the sunset. "He's handsomer than Uncle Dick and lots taller," she thought.

She went to her chest, picked up the little wooden cat from its bed of pink wool, where she now kept it, and stroked the smooth wood softly. She had so little to say when she got home that Sairy Ann was worried.

"You shouldn't stay up there so long weaving," she said. "You'll wear yourself all out, and we aren't in a hurry for that rug."

Meanwhile, Peter, as he walked down the creek, was thinking, "She's got the sparklingest eyes I ever did see."

As the opening of school drew near, "the weavingest girl," as Mammy called her, found herself almost wishing that a flood would come and wash the schoolhouse away, as it had more than a year before. At least a month would be necessary for rebuilding, and she could accomplish so much on her coverlet in that time. After school started, she would have only Saturdays for weaving. However, on second thought, a flood would not help, even if she could order one. The weaving cabin was nearer the creek than the schoolhouse, and it would go first.

Anyway, no flood was forthcoming. The first day of school arrived with the inevitability of such days. Again Lona started out with her dinner pail. Again she said to herself, "Remember Amos." And now she was sustained by the thought of the picture she was making on the old loom. Whatever stupid blunders she might commit in spelling and arithmetic, she knew she had it in her to make beautiful things with her fingers. The coverlet, she felt, was only a beginning. She and Peter together would bring fame to Hollybush Creek.

Chapter 11

The Coverlet Takes a Journey

The redbud bushes were bare of blossoms and leaves. The serviceberries had long ago been eaten by boys and birds. The cardinals' gay whistles were no longer heard from the trees on the ridge top. The dead corn stalks that clothed the steep, side-hill fields were powdered with snow. The creek trail was icy. Still Lona worked at her loom, weaving "Forty-nine Snowballs." All her Saturdays were spent in the weaving cabin now, no matter how bright was the weather or how much Rachel and Jimmy Hayes teased her to come out and play. At last, on a Saturday morning in early February, Mammy Hall helped her unwind from the roller the finished coverlet. They spread it out on Mammy's best bed, and Lona started at once on a run down-creek to fetch Sairy Ann.

"Aunt Sairy," she panted, "Mammy Hall wants to know if you kin come right up."

Sairy Ann almost dropped the pie she held in her hand. "Oh, Lona, is she very sick? What seems to be the matter?"

"She ain't sick. She jest wants to see you right away."

Sairy looked mystified. Whatever could Mammy want in such a hurry to call her away from her morning's work? "All right. You watch these pies and take them out when they are brown."

"Don't put them in yet. She wanted me to come back with you." Lona had no intention of missing the fun of presiding over the showing of the coverlet.

"Curiouser and curiouser," laughed Sairy.

"Look in there on the bed," said Mammy, when Sairy arrived. There were twinkly lights in her deep-set black eyes.

Lona led the way, acting for all the world like Whitenose showing off a new litter of kittens. The "kiver" lay on the old homemade bed, beautiful as soft-tinted sunset clouds.

"What a fine-pretty coverlet," said Sairy, surprised that Mammy should call her up-creek in the midst of Saturday's baking to see a coverlet, no matter how handsome it was.

"Who do you reckon done made that kiver?" asked Mammy.

Light dawned for Sairy Ann. One look at Lona had answered the question. "So this is why you have wanted to spend every Saturday at Mammy's," she said. Then she went up to the bed and looked closely at the pattern. "How beautiful it is! And somehow, it looks like you, Lona."

"It's 'Forty-Nine Snowballs,'" explained Lona, "only they look more like roses in that color. And where you reckon I got the pattern?"

Sairy Ann could not guess.

"Offen that old yeller paper I found in the attic that day. And look at this here," she said, pulling up one corner and showing her name and the year woven there. She had followed the example of Sairy's great-grandmother and of artists who sign and date their canvases.

"That coverlet is going to the State Fair, if I have to walk there with it," announced Sairy.

Lona looked anxious at the thought of anything so precious going out of her sight. "Do you reckon they'd take good care of it and not lose it, nor dirty it, nor nothing?"

"They've got to, and it's going. We can't hide such a light as that under a bushel."

Lona's light was certainly not under a bushel, so far as Hollybush Creek was concerned. Transferred to the house on the ridge, the coverlet lay in state for days while neighbors came to look at it. All the old ladies who had been consulted about drafts came. Aunt Betsy hobbled up to see how the colors came out. Grandma Gayheart asked Peter to bring her down on his mule so that she could see it, and Peter was more than willing.

"You weren't obliged to come, Grandma, nohow," Lona told her. "I was a-going to fetch it up to show you."

"Oh, child, I'm stout enough to git down-creek yet a while."

The old lady was, in fact, glad of an excuse to come and see the household on Wildcat Ridge and have what she called "one of Sairy Ann's fancy dinners." It was a good opportunity to wear her best black dress and to hear all the news on Hollybush Creek. She aimed to stop and see Granny Slone and Aunt Betsy and then go down and stay the night at Peter's house.

Peter looked at the weaving with an eye both more critical and more appreciative than did the old ladies. "I think," he said gravely, "that a girl who can make a kiver as beautiful as that is an artist."

"So do I," agreed Sairy Ann.

Some of the younger women of Hollybush Creek had a different point of view, though they kept it to themselves.

"I can't see," said Lizzie Gayheart to Mattie Boleyn, "why anybody wants to put all that time into making a bed kiver when the store-bought ones is so cheap and so much prettier."

Two weeks later, Lona looked on anxiously while Sairy Ann packed the "Forty-nine Snowballs" in a box, tied it up, and addressed it to "Mrs. Robert Whipple, Clayburgh, Kentucky." Mrs. Whipple, an old friend of Sairy Ann's and Dick's, had offered to arrange for the exhibit of the coverlet at the State Fair.

"What if it gits lost?" asked Lona anxiously. She could hardly bear the thought of sending this precious first fruit of her toil so far away.

"Trust your Uncle Sam; he'll see that it gets there all right," Dick reassured her.

"S'posen Bije loses it offen the wagon, and it goes into the creek. S'posen the box busts open, and the kiver gits torn—"

"Oh, stop your supposens!" broke in Sairy Ann. "Don't you know that you have to take chances in order to do anything in life?"

Lona carried the box down the ridge trail and waited for the arrival of Bije. She had insisted on personally conducting the package thus far on its journey.

"Take special care of it, won't you?" she begged the glum old mail carrier and explained how important the package was. "It will be all right," said Bije, carelessly tossing the box into the wagon, just as if, thought Lona, it was only an ordinary piece of mail. She watched the wagon jolting along the creek till it disappeared through Paw-Paw Gap, as though she were taking leave of a dear friend.

Lona had no peace of mind until word came from Clayburgh more than a week later that the coverlet had arrived unharmed. Now she worried lest someone steal it. Sairy Ann declared that Lona acted exactly like a mother whose baby had been taken from her.

Meanwhile, the coverlet had traveled on two trains and had been left by the postman at a rather handsome house in Clayburgh, "down in the Bluegrass." It now hung like a great wall painting in the exhibition hall on the State Fairgrounds, just outside the city. In that display of beautiful things sent there from all over the state, Lona's "Forty-nine Snowballs" more than held its own.

On the last day of the fair, two men and a woman stood discussing the patchwork bed quilts, the coverlets, the pillow tops, the jams and the jellies that filled the hall. Up and down the room they went, with critical expressions on their faces, looking, feeling, smelling, tasting. Sometimes they stood for a long time before a piece of work. Again they passed by quickly.

The other people in the room watched every movement and every glance of the three judges. In their hands lay the fates of those who had brought here the best of their year's work.

"That lady tasted Mrs. Bates's piccalilli three times," noted one spectator.

"They've been looking at my bed quilt for fifteen minutes. Do you suppose—?" The excited exhibitor did not finish the question.

"I'll bet they have looked at that coverlet six times. They keep coming back to it," observed another. "It certainly is a beauty, and do you notice the label? It says that the girl who wove it is only fifteen years old—a mountain girl, too."

"You don't say so. I call that pretty smart!"

Excitement ran high as it became evident that the choice for first prize lay between the "Forty-nine Snowballs" coverlet in the corner and the "Flower Pot" patchwork quilt, hung conspicuously opposite the entrance. Would the judges ever stop walking back and forth between those two pieces of work? Ah! They had decided. One of the gentlemen was leaning over and pinning "First Prize" right in the middle of the "Forty-nine Snowballs."

Two days later, back on Hollybush Creek, an excited girl was opening an envelope addressed to her marked, "Registered." It was the first letter she had ever received. In the envelope was a note from Mrs. Whipple. From the folds of the letter there fell a crisp ten-dollar bill.

Lona stared at the note and at the money.

"What does it say, Lona?" asked Sairy Ann eagerly.

Lona could not speak. She could only read the written

words over and over and feel of the crackling bill in a daze. Sairy Ann patiently waited for the girl to come to, as one waits for a person who has fainted to revive. Finally, Lona said slowly, as though she did not quite believe it, "My kiver took the first prize—and it's ten dollars."

She handed the letter to Sairy Ann, who read it through. "Oh, Lona, I'm mighty proud of you. And isn't it wonderful that Mrs. Whipple wants to buy it!"

"To buy it?"

"Why, yes, didn't you read the letter?"

"I reckon I didn't git clear to the end."

"Forty dollars!" Lona's eyes grew enormous as she read. "But I couldn't sell it, noways," she said. "I'm a-going to keep it always and hand it down to my children and grandchildren, jest like Abigail Hughes handed hers down to Mammy Hall. And my grandchildren are a-going to say, 'Grandma wove it when she was fifteen years old, and it took the first prize at the State Fair.'"

"Couldn't you weave another for yourself and your grandchildren?"

"I reckon I could make another for her, but she can't have that one. Not noways."

Suddenly, Sairy Ann realized how much the coverlet meant to Lona.

Again Lona brewed strange-smelling mixtures in Aunt Betsy's iron pot and made the elderberry bushes blossom with skeins of colored yarn hung out to dry. Again the cabin heard the clackety-clack of her loom and her happy voice singing:

> *"With perfect delight,*
> *By day and by night,*
> *This wonderful song I'll sing."*

Chapter 12

Lona Tries to Write a Letter

One Saturday in September, as Lona was making her shuttle fly to and fro across the loom, Peter stopped at the cabin door.

"What! Have you sold another?" he asked as he noticed the beginnings of a new coverlet in the loom. Like everyone else on the creek, he had heard how Lona's coverlet had taken the prize and how a lady from the level country wanted to buy it.

"No, jest one, but I couldn't sell my prize kiver; I'm going to keep it always. So I'm making another like it fer the furrin lady."

Peter smiled. "I know. That's the way I feel about some of the things I've made."

He stood watching her for a few moments with a grave expression on his face. "I'm a-going away tomorrow," he said.

Lona sat up with a jerk and broke her yarn in two. Then she bent very low over the loom to splice it. "Where you a-going?" she asked after a long silence.

"To Clayburgh, to that school I told you about."

There was no sparkle in Lona's eyes now. "Clear to the level country," she said. If he had told her he was going to China or

Lona of Hollybush Creek

Australia, it would not have seemed any farther away. "When you aim to come back?"

"Christmas time for a vacation, maybe."

"I wish Christmas was next week." Lona looked down at her loom as she spoke.

"I wish it was tomorrow," said Peter, "but I don't guess it's going to make us feel any better to talk about it anymore. I'll write to you—that is, if you'd like for me to."

Lona smiled for the first time since Peter had told her his news. "'Course, I'd like it."

He took her small right hand, shuttle and all, and gave it a squeeze. "Goodbye, little prizewinner! Keep on weaving," he said soberly. Then he strode across the worn threshold and went down the creek trail as fast as though he were taking the train that morning.

What a long way from Hollybush he was going, thought Peter. Why, it took Bije's mules and two trains to get him there!

Lona began to weave at a furious speed. Twice she broke her yarn and had to stop and knot it.

Peter's first letter was an event. It was not only the first time a boy had written to Lona, it was the first time anyone had written her a letter, except for the business note about the coverlet.

Dear Lona,

Cities are funny places. I don't see what folks want to live all huddled up together for, making each other plumb deaf with their noises, covering up all the green grass with pavements, and making lights so bright it's like daytime all night.

I wish I could hear Hollybush Creek talking to itself. I wish I could look into your cabin and see what you are doing.

Reckon I'm just homesick and will get over it in another week. Anyway, I like school. I'm taking drawing and clay modeling. They're both fun, but there never was so much fun doing anything as there is in feeling things take shape, almost take life, out of clay.

Write to me soon and tell me all the Hollybush news and what you are doing.
Your friend Peter

It was a beautiful letter, Lona thought. It sounded just like Peter talking. She read it over at least five times the day it came and placed it with the little wooden cat. In the days that followed, she unfolded and refolded the letter so many times that the creases in the paper became slits. However, this caused no difficulty in rereading, for by that time, she knew the words by heart.

Although it had been a joy to receive the letter, there was agony in trying to answer it. "I never kin write a fine letter like that," she said to herself despairingly as she sat in her bedroom chewing the end of a pen. How did one even begin? How could one make words on paper sound natural?

Dear Peter,
I received your letter. My kiver is half done.

There was prolonged and feverish pen chewing, during which a blob of ink fell from her pen and landed splishily in the middle of the page. Lona took a fresh sheet of paper and began again:

Dear Peter,
I received your letter. My kiver is half done. I wish I could shew it to you.

She chewed the abused pen handle for fully fifteen minutes but could not think of anything more to say, so signed herself:

Your friend Lona

She read the short letter over, tore it up, and threw it into the wastebasket. It sounded like a little girl's letter, and here she was fifteen, going on sixteen. A boy who had been through high school and was studying in the city would laugh at a letter like that.

After a few days, she made another try, with no better results. This time there were tears in her eyes when she tore the paper into fine pieces. Would she ever learn to write letters that sounded nice? Anyhow, she was not going to send him one of her foolish scrawls, with mistakes that would make him laugh at her and show him what a little ignoramus she was. No, never! Why, he wouldn't have anything more to do with her if he knew she couldn't write any better than that. He had said he might come home for Christmas. She would wait till she could talk to him. Funny how much easier it was to talk things than to write them.

A second letter came from Peter about two weeks after the first. It consisted of three questions:

Dear Lona,
Did you get my other letter? Are you all right? Why don't you write to me?
Your friend Peter

Again Lona got out pen and ink bottle. She would write a few words, anyway, so that he would know she got his letter. Again she chewed the pen handle frantically, and again she tore up the labored, blotted, misspelled result, afraid to send it lest Peter should stop liking her when he saw how little she knew compared to him. If only she could ask Sairy Ann or Dick to help her! But that was simply impossible. Somehow she felt shyer than she had ever felt before about this friendship with Peter. She felt like keeping it all to herself and telling no one about it, just as she had never shown the wooden cat to anyone.

Sairy Ann noticed that the letters from the city had stopped coming as suddenly as they had begun to arrive. She also noticed that Lona was unnaturally solemn.

"What do you hear from Peter?" she asked Lona one day.

"Nothing lately."

"Don't you write to him?"

"No, I don't have time to write letters, noways." Lona's tone was one of extreme indifference. Not for worlds would she have told anyone, not even her Aunt Sairy, how much she liked Peter and how hard she had tried to write a letter.

"She'll be the most heartless flirt on the creek when she's a little older," thought Sairy Ann, and she said no more about Peter.

Pity that Lona could not have used television, as she bent over the loom in her cabin. She would have seen a lonely young man watching the mails, the sober look in his gray eyes turning into a hurt look as the days went by, and he decided that the girl had forgotten all about him. He thought of the talks they had had in the old cabin, of the confidences they had exchanged about hopes and plans for the future. He recalled the birthday party more than a year before. He could see Lona now as, pink-cheeked and sparkling-eyed, she had danced the Virginia Reel with him that night. Suddenly he realized how much she had come to mean to him in those few talks they had had together.

The words of the old song sounded in his ears:

> *"Big dog bark and little one bite you,*
> *Hey ho, diddle dum dee-ay.*
> *Big gal'll court and little one'll slight you,*
> *Heigh ho, diddle dum dee-ay."*

"I don't care if Lona never writes to me or speaks to me again," he said bitterly. But it was a lie, and he knew it. "I'll get me another girl, and it won't be a little black-eyed girl."

Chapter 13

Lona Opens a Bank Account

Lona had expected the money for her coverlet would be crackly new bills, like the State Fair prize. Instead, it was only a piece of paper with "forty dollars" marked on it. Uncle Dick said it was just as good as money, but somehow it did not seem the same at all. He took her to Blairstown on Twinkle. She carried in her purse the check, the ten-dollar prize money and the four dollars Dick had paid her last year for the rag rug. When they rode home, the saddlebag held a small book, proof that Lona Allen had deposited to her account in the Blairstown Savings Bank fifty-four dollars. It seemed to the mountain girl an enormous sum. She wished she could see it in silver or, better yet, gold pieces and pile it up in front of her and handle it.

News of the money Lona had made took wings and flew up-creek and down. The amount grew in the telling—from forty dollars to fifty, from fifty to seventy-five, from seventy-five to a hundred. Even Lizzie Gayheart and Mattie Boleyn were impressed. "I'd weave one of them old kivers if someone would pay me a hundred dollars," said Lizzie. "That woman must have been plumb out of her head to do it," Mattie decided.

Lona found great joy in thinking how she might spend her sudden wealth. A dress for her Aunt Sairy of blue silk—the color of her eyes. A red necktie for Uncle Dick. (Lona had a special fondness for red neckties.) A doll carriage for Gail's doll to take the place of the rude wooden cart Preacher Johnny had made for her. For herself, she would buy a red coat with a gray fur collar. One of the teachers at the Slone's Creek High School had a coat like that, and Lona had often longed to try it on. She had no idea how much of her fifty-four dollars would be left after these purchases had been made, but she would have to save enough to buy something for Mammy Hall and for Aunt Betsy. Without them, there would never have been any coverlet. Anyway, it was better not to be in a hurry about spending the money. Aunt Sairy and Uncle Dick said to save it and keep adding a little to it. Then perhaps she could go away to school sometime. This suggestion had little appeal for Lona. She could get all the "book learnin'" she wanted at the Hollybush School.

"You'll have to get a secretary pretty soon to take care of your mail," joked Dick the day a letter came addressed to Lona Allen in a strange handwriting. This time a friend of Mrs. Whipple's wrote to ask if Lona would weave a "Forty-nine Snowballs" coverlet for her, just like the one she had made for Mrs. Whipple, except hers was to be green and white. She would expect to pay the same price as Lona had been paid before.

The lumbering old loom was threaded again and the fires were kindled under Aunt Betsy's iron kettle. This time Lona picked indigo from Mammy's garden and gathered hickory shells. She wondered how those black old shells and a weed could possibly make a pretty color, but when the yarn came out of the kettle, it was the beautiful deep green she wanted.

And now Lona wove every minute she could possibly squeeze out of a week, even hanging lanterns from the time-blackened beams and weaving by their pale light. Once Dick had to come after her and fairly drag her home at eight o'clock in the evening; she had worked right through the supper hour without realizing it. The thought that she could make lovely things with her own hands for which the people in that far-off level country would pay her fairly intoxicated her.

Sometimes she would look at the little wooden cat and wish she could tell Peter about her good fortune and show him how the "Forty-nine Snowballs" looked in green and white. He was, it seemed to her, in another world now.

Chapter 14

Lona Forgets Her Lines

Christmas was a time of great joy for the boys and girls on Hollybush Creek. There was always a celebration at the school, a celebration that included stripping presents from the largest tree that could be squeezed through the schoolhouse door. Thanks to the efforts of the school teacher, Sairy Ann, Dick, and the Slone's Creek Community Center, no boy or girl went away empty-handed. And there were often special gifts for the oldest inhabitants.

The house on Wildcat Ridge was the busiest place for miles around during the days before Christmas. There were the presents from Slone's Creek to be packed over on the bony backs of Whitey and Pappy Hall's mule, Blackbird. Those presents and others sent in from the level country had to be wrapped, tied with bright ribbons, and labeled. Then there were the specials for the sick—a cup of custard with a leaf of holly laid across the top or a piece of fruit covered with silver paper and tied with a splashing red bow.

Yards of popcorn strings would be needed to decorate the school tree and the small tree that Dick would cut and place in a corner of the living room on the ridge. And after all these things and more had been done, Sairy Ann and Mammy Hall would cook chicken and biscuits and pies enough to feed Granny Slone, Preacher Johnny and his wife, Mammy and Pappy Hall, and Rachel, in addition to the regular family.

Lona was especially excited about Christmas this year. The school was giving a play, and she had the leading part—a snow maiden dressed in sparkling, frosty white from the top of her head to her toes. The property boxes and old-clothes boxes at the Slone's Creek School had been ransacked for materials for her costume. From an old white flannel coat, cotton batting, a few bits of white fur, and much artificial snow, Lona had made herself an outfit that might have been imported straight from the polar regions.

"How do I look?" she asked Sairy Ann and Dick, when finally she stood all in shimmering white. "Fine, just like a snow lady," they said, but both were thinking, "How lovely she is!" She was indeed dazzling. The glistening white set off the darkness of her eyes and brows and the deep pink of her cheeks and brought out all the eager aliveness of her small being. She took a good look at herself in the glass in her room and decided that she did look pretty. But she had no idea how beautiful a snow maiden she really was.

"I think," said Lona, as she and Sairy Ann strung popcorn ropes in the kitchen together, "that this is going to be the nicest Christmas I've ever had."

She did not ask herself the reason for this opinion. If she had, perhaps a voice within her would have said, "Because Peter is coming home and will be here in time for the school tree." Grandma Gayheart had told the good news to Sairy Ann that afternoon. She wondered if Peter would think she was pretty in her snow costume. And what would he say when he saw the new green-and-white coverlet that was growing on her loom?

Over and over, Lona rehearsed her lines—to her reflection in the looking glass, to Sairy Ann, to Dick, to the teacher. It was a long part, and she must know it perfectly. It would not do to falter or blunder on this, her first appearance—and in the leading role, too. Even weaving was forgotten for all of two weeks.

On the evening of the celebration, Lona watched through a hole in the curtain while the schoolroom filled with men, women, children, and babies from all up and down Hollybush Creek, from Coon Hollow and even from Bull Creek. Some were faces she saw every day—Preacher Johnny's, Granny Slone's, Bud Hayes'. Other visitors were almost strangers, so seldom did they ride their bony mules down to Hollybush from lonely cabins up the hollows and branches. Finally, she saw Peter come in with his mother and Grandma Gayheart and Mary Hayes.

Lona began helping frantically behind the scenes. She was a jealous little fool, she supposed, but she couldn't bear to watch Peter laughing and talking so steadily with Mary. Did he like Mary? Did he like Mary better than he did her? Had he forgotten all about her? Over and over the questions kept asking themselves.

The curtain was pulled aside to reveal Lona in white on a snowy throne, in the center of a stage glistening with artificial snow. The audience burst into loud clapping and foot-stamping. There were calls of "It's Lona," "It's Lona." The snow maiden stole a glance at Peter. He was not clapping. He did not seem to be even looking at her.

She sat on her throne, unable to remember a word of the part she had learned so perfectly. The voice of the teacher prompting her came from behind a curtain. Lona did not hear her. The teacher raised her voice, frantic lest Lona spoil the show by having stage fright. People began to clear their throats nervously. Making a terrific effort to remember what she was doing, she began haltingly to say the opening lines.

Then all at once, the words came back with a rush. She

was no longer Lona Allen. She stole no more glances toward the corner where Peter sat. She was the snow maiden and the leading lady of the play. No more promptings were necessary. An enraptured audience watched her and listened to her clear voice. When it was over, the cast had to give curtain call after curtain call. They shouted, "Lona! Lona!" With eyes like Christmas candles and cheeks like holly berries, she came out by herself and bowed. Peter looked at the ceiling.

At the end, the whole school stood on the stage and sang Christmas carols.

> *"It came upon the midnight clear,*
> *That glorious song of old,"*

sang Lona with the others. There was proud defiance and no Christmas spirit at all in her tone.

> *"Holy night, peaceful night.*
> *All is calm. All is bright."*

But all was not calm and bright for the girl in white.

The curtains were pulled down to reveal the tree amid "Oh's" and "Ah's" of delight over its beauty and anticipation of what was to come. A jingle of bells sounded and in came Dick, bearded almost to the eyes with white cotton and padded with pillows till he looked like a fat old Santa Claus. "It's the doctor," "It's Doctor Dick," shouted the children.

Then began the really important business of the day—the filling of the children's hands with "pretties" and sweets. Lona, still in her snow costume, flew about distributing the gifts. "Grandma Gayheart," called out Dick, handing a package to Lona. Grandma was one of the few old people who was always remembered.

Lona looked about for someone else to deliver the gift, but all the others were busy. How she wished she didn't have to go

Then began the really important business of the day—the filling of the children's hands with "pretties" and sweets.

over to that corner. She dashed over to the old lady as though she were in a terrible rush. Peter looked up. "Howdy, Peter," she said. "Howdy, Lona," he replied stiffly and gravely, then turned quickly and went on talking to Mary. Lona was on the other side of the room as though she had flown there.

She rushed about with gifts the rest of the evening, like a mechanical tool that had been wound up and could not stop. She did not want to think. She was afraid she would burst out crying if she stood still and thought for one moment, and nobody must ever know how unhappy she was about Peter and Mary—nobody.

Preacher Johnny, as he rode home on his mule with "his woman" up behind, prophesied a sad end for Lona. "No good will come o' deckin' herself out that-a-way and play-actin'. Sairy Ann calls it tableaux—whatever them are—but it's play-actin', and play-actin' is of the devil."

"She even painted her face, I reckon," said his wife, Maria, in shocked tones.

Granny Slone was sure that "Lona would git vain and full o' sinful pride if they didn't stop dressin' her up like a doll."

"And I thought this was a-going to be the nicest Christmas I ever done had," Lona said to herself bitterly as she cried into her pillow on Christmas night long after everyone else was asleep. Anyway, she was glad Christmas was over. She had play-acted all day, pretending to have as much fun as ever over the contents of her stocking, the family tree, and the fried chicken dinner.

She even had to listen while Peter was discussed at the dinner table and to act as though she were not interested. "Looks like Peter Gayheart was aimin' to marry Mary," Preacher Johnny had said. The older people on Hollybush thought a girl and a boy were as good as engaged if they went out anywhere together. But Granny Slone, as usual, knew more than anyone else did.

"I don't guess so," she had said. "His grandma told me he had a girl down in the Bluegrass. They all takes to furriners when they goes out o' the mountains." Then she had shot a sly look at Sairy Ann, for Dick, too, was a "furriner," as Hollybush used the word.

Lona had pretended to be so busy with a chicken leg that she didn't hear a word the old folks were saying. But it had seemed as though every mouthful would choke her.

"He's a flirt, the worst kind of a flirt," she told Whitenose, who slept soundly in her box beside the bed. "He's got a girl on Hollybush and a girl in the level country, and he's forgotten all about me." Whitenose woke with a start as something wet splashed on her nose, gave a "p-r-rup" of surprise, and curled up a little tighter.

Poor silly Lona! She was too inexperienced in making and keeping friends, too childish for her years, and too self-centered to realize that by not answering Peter's letters she had deliberately sacrificed his friendship to her own sensitiveness and false pride. She had no idea what she had done.

The day after Christmas, Lona went up to the weaving cabin. Shivering with cold, she built a fire on the hearth that had been fireless for more than a week. Then she went to her chest, pulled out the little carved cat and dropped it into the hottest flames.

"Oh, child," said Mammy Hall when she looked in on her a little later. "What a clatter you do make with that loom! Sounds like you was aimin' to tear it all to pieces."

Chapter 15

To a "Furrin" Land

Again Lona jolted down to Blairstown over the stony creek road with Bije. Under the seat lay a large suitcase. This time Blairstown was only the first stage of a long journey of a day and a night that involved eating and sleeping on a train. The journey's end was a large city in that great world that waited out beyond the mountains. Lona had heard many tales of those "furrin" cities—how there were houses as high as Wildcat Ridge and so many cars and so many people rushing around there had to be a policeman on every corner with a club and a gun to keep order.

The new silk dress Lona had made for herself was what is called a "daring" print. The new hat sported a devil-may-care bow, fashioned by the deft hand of Sairy Ann. But even this raiment did not impart a brave or dashing appearance to the traveler. She was scared and homesick and looked it.

Yes, now, before Bije had reached the headwaters of Big Creek, homesickness had set in. She looked back at the soft blue hills that folded against one another to fill the gap. She raised her eyes to the hillside, where full-blown laurel was like drifts of pale pink snow, and she could hardly restrain herself from telling Bije to stop the mules and let her go back.

"Stop being a baby; you're going to be sixteen years old next month," she reminded herself sternly. But the reminder produced no effect on her feelings. Bije, the silent, was so moved by her miserable aspect that he actually began to talk. His remarks were not exactly reassuring.

"You'll have to take care o' yourself. Somebody, like as not, will try to kidnap ye. They tell how gals jest drop out o' sight down thar, and nobody knows where they're done gone— thousands o' them spirited away every year. And it's the gals from the country they lays fer. They can spot 'em at sight."

"I kin take care of myself," said Lona in an unconvincingly weak tone of voice.

"That's what they all say, I reckon."

Lona decided to let the conversation die a natural death at this point. Her thoughts, gloomy as they were, seemed cheerful compared with Bije's talk. She began to concentrate on the directions Sairy Ann had given her. First, she would take the two o'clock train at Blairstown and go to the end of the line. Then she would ask a porter to put her on the five-forty train and give him ten cents for carrying her bag.

"Have a good supper in the dining car," Sairy Ann advised, "and ask the porter to make up your bed whenever you feel sleepy." In the morning, she would be in the great city, and she was to wait by the magazine stand in the waiting room till she saw a man with blue eyes and gray hair wearing a light gray suit with a lily-of-the-valley in his buttonhole.

What would he be like—that man in the gray suit? So much depended on that. He was to teach her to weave on an eight-harness loom and to show her new patterns and new ways of making and setting dyes. In other words, she had graduated from the Granny-Hall-Aunt-Betsy School of Weaving.

All this had come about through the "Forty-nine Snowballs." Those two coverlets had gone out of the mountains and brought back to the weaver more than money. They had earned for her the interest of people a thousand miles away. Their interest had resulted in an offer from the gray-suited man to teach her, during his vacation, what he knew about handweaving—and that was much, it seemed.

Mr. Gregory was the man's name. He was a teacher of manual training and handcrafts. The old-time home industries were his hobby. After much letter writing, it had been arranged that Lona was to spend the summer in his home in the suburbs of a Northern city and be his pupil.

She didn't know she was fond of old Bije. Yet when the train pulled out of Blairstown and she watched his familiar figure retreating down the platform, the pent-up tears ran down her cheeks. She took a determined but entirely affected interest in the scenery, to prevent her fellow passengers from seeing those tears. She did not turn round when the conductor took her ticket, but he seemed to see right through the back of her head. "I reckon everything's going to be all right, after ye gits used to it," he said in a soothing tone.

Now she was lying in the strangest kind of a bed made out of two seats by the colored porter's magic. Within her head, pictures of new sights went round and round in a dizzy panorama, and her body fairly ached with novel sensations. She lay wide awake in her berth, listening to the engine and sniffing eagerly the soft scent of honeysuckle the night winds blew into the train. Thank goodness they had not left all the honeysuckle behind yet. She was sure she was not going to sleep a wink all night and was almost afraid to let herself, lest something dreadful happen to her. As a matter of fact, she was the first person in the car to lose consciousness, so tired were her small body and over-active brain after so strange a day.

Would the man in the gray suit be there by the magazine stand? This was the first question she asked herself when she heard the porter calling, "Seven o'clock, Miss." A look out the window made her wild with anxiety lest they miss connections. Gone were green fields. Gone were the trees. Gone was the sky. There were only walls of brick and stone, and streets of stone, and a network of wires.

The railroad station was a city in itself. It was at least a mile to the waiting room, thought Lona as she tugged her suitcase in the direction the crowd was going. And what a palace of a place! The girl from Hollybush Creek looked up in utter amazement at the tall stone pillars and vaulted roof. Crash! Thud! She was down on her knees on the hard stone floor. Her suitcase was lying flat on its side a yard away from her. "Why don't you look where you're going?" It was the voice of the woman over whose bag she had fallen, while her gaze had been fixed on the ceiling. How crisp and hard it sounded to a girl used to the soft accents of mountain speech!

"Are you hurt?" asked another voice—a kind voice. She looked up from her knees to see a man picking up the suitcase and holding out a hand to help her. She scrambled to her feet and looked into the face of a gray-suited man who wore a lily-of-the-valley in his buttonhole.

"I'm all right," she said, feeling of her aching knees and convinced that not a quarter of an inch of whole skin remained on them. Mr. Gregory smiled. It was a little like Uncle Dick's smile, thought Lona, only of course not nearly so nice. "I didn't expect you'd go down on your knees to me so soon as this, Miss Lona Allen," he said.

Lona burst out laughing, and immediately her knees felt better. Mr. Gregory joined in. The ice was completely broken. They chatted together like old friends as they breakfasted in the station. "That was a good description of you Mrs. Lawrence sent me. I recognized you at once, even on your knees," said Mr. Gregory.

"And I knew 'twas you when I see the lily-of-the-valley."

He grinned. "Now I hope you aren't going to associate me always with lilies-of-the-valley. It doesn't seem a very manly emblem."

"I won't if you'll fergit about me falling on my knees to you."

"It's a bargain. And what's more, I won't tell anyone about it, either. And now it's time to take the train."

"The train?" asked Lona in surprise, for she thought her journey was over.

"We live out in the suburbs," explained Mr. Gregory— which was no explanation at all for Lona; she had never heard of suburbs.

"Mrs. Lawrence wrote me that you were sixteen; that's just the age of my daughter, Janet," said Mr. Gregory, when they were seated on the train. Lona was overjoyed at the thought of having a companion of her own age.

"Timothy and Bob, the twins, are twelve. They'll probably be shy and keep out of your way at first, and then, when they get acquainted, will tease you and bother you to death. But you look as though you would be a match for them. So you see," he added, "you don't have to worry about getting lonesome at our house."

When they reached Arden, Lona decided that suburbs were the same as a city, except that the houses were not so tall and had patches of grass around them.

"I'm so glad you have come to stay with us," said Mrs. Gregory, who met them at the door. "I've heard about you and the Lawrences from my friend Mrs. Whipple, down in Clayburgh, where we used to live. Now I shall have a chance to get firsthand news from Hollybush Creek."

One couldn't help feeling a little bit at home with the Gregorys, thought Lona, even in such strange surroundings. Though their home was simple, it seemed to the mountain girl a place of grandeur. How high the rooms were! How shiny the floors! How beautiful the rugs and pictures! Yet it did not seem half so pleasant as the house on Wildcat Ridge. The bed in her room was soft and springy, the cushioned chair inviting, and the framed pictures on the wall were lovely. But how quickly Lona would have exchanged the bed for her own harder, lumpier one, with its red-and-white patchwork quilt and Whitenose's box beneath; the armchair for her cushionless hickory one made by Preacher Johnny; the framed pictures for the beloved colored pictures she had cut out of old magazines and pasted on the walls.

Lona had not been in the house long before Mr. Gregory took her up to the big top-floor room he called his shop. This, she decided, was the pleasantest room in the house. She was glad she was going to do her weaving here. There were two looms in the room, a carpenter's bench and tools, bits of wood in the various stages of their evolution into furniture, baskets finished and partly finished, sheets of iron and copper and brass. There were even lumps of silver and semi-precious stones in the process of being made into jewelry.

How Peter would love this place! That, to Lona's surprise, was her first thought as she looked about the room. She had made up her mind to forget about Peter. She had not allowed herself even to think about him for months. Now here he was right back in her mind again. Well, he needn't think he was going to stay. She had enough to think about now without bothering with him.

"What fine-pretty weaving!" she said, a little wistfully, as she looked around the walls. They were almost completely covered with woven pieces in patterns ancient and modern, some faded and worn, some bright and new. Mr. Gregory looked pleased as he watched the girl's delighted gaze. "So you like my picture gallery?"

"Oh, yes, sir! It makes me want to start weaving right away."

"You shall this afternoon, if you want to."

He went around the room with her, telling something interesting about each woven piece. "This one came from your own mountains. This I bought from a toothless old lady in Sweden. Here is something one of my pupils wove." Lona became so interested that she was sorry when Mrs. Gregory called that lunch was ready.

To Lona's disappointment, Janet did not appear at luncheon. She was off on a picnic, it seemed. "I sometimes wonder if I have a daughter," said Mrs. Gregory, with a smile. "I so seldom see her." Lona puzzled over this remark. Where did Janet spend her time? She knew nothing of the parties and the sports with which the young people of the level country were occupied.

Timothy and Bob did little during the meal but nudge each other and giggle, much to the embarrassment of their parents. Finally, they were sent away from the table in disgrace, red-faced and choking over their food. Lona did not connect their behavior with herself until the horrible truth was forced upon her. At Mrs. Gregory's suggestion, she went up to her room after lunch to try to sleep off the effects from the journey. Finding herself too wide awake to follow this advice, she stepped out onto a balcony immediately over the back porch. From below floated up the voices of Mrs. Gregory and the twins.

"If you ever act like that during a meal again, you will not be allowed to eat with the family while she is here."

"But, Mom, we couldn't help it; she talks so funny! 'It's a right-smart,' and 'I didn't reckon I'd sleep any bit, nohow.'" They imitated her voice and accents exactly.

"But that's the way people talk where she comes from. We may sound just as funny to her, and she may have felt like laughing at us. Besides, you must remember that she hasn't had a chance to go to school very much."

Lona's face flushed crimson. She went quickly to her room, threw herself down on her bed, and cried till she fell asleep from exhaustion.

At dinner, Mrs. Gregory noticed that Lona's eyelids were swollen and decided that the poor girl must be very homesick. Her efforts to be particularly nice to her made Lona feel the more unhappy. "She's sorry for the ignorant girl from Hollybush Creek," she thought bitterly. As for the twins, they ate in a silence that was noticeably unnatural.

Janet put in her appearance at breakfast the next morning. It did not seem possible to Lona that this tall, poised girl with her sophisticated makeup and manner could be exactly the same age as herself. Janet was thinking, "How like a child she seems!" But she said, "It's going to be fun to have you here. Mother says you are just my age." Then she began trying to discover what she had in common with this queer little person.

"Do you play tennis?"

Lona said that she didn't. She had heard that there was such a game, but she hadn't the faintest idea how it was played.

"Or golf?" Janet was as ignorant of what people did in the mountains as Lona was of modern suburban life.

"Play what?"

"Golf," repeated Janet, with growing amazement. "You play it with clubs and little balls."

"I reckon I never done heard of that game before."

"Well, we can go swimming together."

Lona had to admit with increasing embarrassment that she could not swim. Janet gave up the struggle and devoted herself to breakfast.

Mrs. Gregory came to the rescue. "Lona can do a great many things you cannot do, Janet," she said, "things much more useful than golf or tennis. She does beautiful handweaving and makes her own dresses, and I'm going to ask her to teach Mary how to cook spoon bread and fried chicken that will make your mouth water."

"Aren't you wonderful!" said Janet, but the words lacked the ring of sincerity, and Lona knew it. Both girls felt uncomfortable.

Chapter 16

Homesick for Hollybush

The first week at Arden was the longest week of Lona's life. Not an hour passed that her thoughts did not go back to Hollybush Creek. "I wonder if Aunt Sairy and Uncle Dick are up yet?" she asked herself when she first woke up in the morning. At noon, she longed for a dinner of fatback and cornbread on Wildcat Ridge, instead of the dainty luncheon served at the Gregorys'. In the evening, she would shut her eyes and listen in imagination to the murmur of the creek and to the "plinkety-plink" of Bud Hayes' homemade banjo. Every night in her dreams, she went home to ride old Whitey, to play with Gail, to weave in her cabin, to talk with Mammy Hall and Sairy and Dick. Waking was a bewildering coming-back to the realities, or rather, the unrealities, of her new world.

The first letter from Sairy Ann was worn ragged, so many times did she read it. Sairy told of Gail's latest cute sayings and how she kept asking where Lona was, how they were holding the baby clinic twice a week now, of Granny Slone's losing her favorite pipe and how Dick had bought her a new one, and all the gossip of the creek. Lona answered by return mail, even though letter writing was still hard labor for her; then she hung about the front door watching for the postman every morning until she received an answer.

She liked the Gregorys but did not feel really at home with them. Mr. and Mrs. Gregory were kind but very busy. She could not share in the merry life of Janet, who was always going somewhere. The twins, too, led an absorbing life of their own with a crowd of neighborhood boys. Only at her loom in the big, top-floor room was the lonely girl happy. During those first days, she plied her shuttle till her back ached and her arms were almost numb. Thus she could ease a little that aching longing for home.

"You're the first pupil I ever had who didn't know enough to quit working," said Mr. Gregory one day, fairly pulling her off her chair. "Come on now, Mrs. Gregory and I are going for a drive, and you are coming with us."

Lona had ridden in a car only a few times in her life, and then over stony, mud-rutted roads. This gliding along smooth-surfaced roads seemed like flying. And now, for the first time, she saw and heard the sea! She had sung of the sea in old mountain ballads. She had seen it in movies, dashing ships to pieces and buffeting swimmers. At last, its wonder was before her eyes. She could only stare and say over and over, "How beautiful! How beautiful!"

Lona's eager interest in this drive led to other invitations. The Gregorys delighted in her fresh enthusiasm and her amusing remarks. "Where'd they git all these flat stones?" she asked as they rolled along the cement road. "Do they have play-parties every day in this town?" This was her comment on the number of "dressed-up ladies" they saw on their drives. Mr. Gregory was convulsed when she asked, "Is he a gangster?" as a harmless-looking hitchhiker held out his hand to hail them.

Never would she forget the first time she went to a motion-picture theater with Mrs. Gregory. Movies she had seen at the Slone's Creek Community Center and at the Hollybush School, but this was the first time she had seen the inside of a theater. "Jest like a palace, ain't it?" she said, looking around at the mural decorations and gilt chairs in the lobby. "Isn't it?" she corrected herself quickly. The twins' laughter had accomplished what the combined efforts of Sairy and Dick for nearly five years had failed to do—made her wish to speak correctly.

In the picture, Lona lost herself completely. "Oh! He's going to get kilt," her agonized cry rang out at a tense moment. A dozen people turned to stare at her. "Sh-h-h!" sounded in her ear from someone behind her. She was glad it was dark so that no one could see her blushes. Arden audiences and Hollybush Creek audiences were evidently different. She realized this again on Sunday when she went to church with the Gregorys. "The preacher did all the talking," she remarked in disappointed tones at the dinner table.

"Why, who does the talking in your church?" asked Janet.

Lona described a Sunday meeting at the Hollybush schoolhouse, where Preacher Johnny merely started the ball rolling and everyone who felt moved to talk, or even to shout and sing, jumped to his feet and did so.

"How funny!" said Janet.

"No funnier than your meeting seems to me," replied Lona, who was beginning to feel less shy and more like asserting herself.

The radio fascinated the mountain girl. She especially liked to be left alone with it so that she could turn the dial as much as she pleased, mixing dance music with news reports, and opera with comic dialogue. It was all part of getting acquainted with this strange new world. Sometimes, when quite sure no one was around, she would practice dance steps as she had seen Janet do or imitate a crooner. By the end of her second week, Hollybush was less in her thoughts. The level country was not so bad, after all.

"Mother, she'd be a flat tire at a beach party. She can't swim, and she talks like a Fiji Islander. She'd ask dumb questions and embarrass me to tears. I won't have her."

"Now, Janet, you can't leave her out in the cold all the time.

Her guardians are good friends of one of my best friends, and we're going to give her a pleasant summer. Besides, she's the most interesting young person I've met in a long time."

"Why, Mother!" was all the amazed Janet could answer to this last remark.

Fortunately, Lona heard none of this conversation. Otherwise, she would not have had such a blissful time jumping breakers in a borrowed bathing suit and roasting hot dogs over glowing coals on the beach. To be sure, she could not swim with the other young people, and much of their slangy wisecracking was utterly unintelligible to her.

But Lona had a great capacity for fun, and when her first shyness wore off, no one was more fun than she. In the water and in the drying-off races and ball-throwing on the beach, she was like some hilarious sprite that has come out of her wild haunts into a company of mere mortals and is having a lark with them.

"Isn't she cute!" said the girls a little patronizingly.

"That mountain kid is fun, even if she hasn't much of a line of talk," agreed the boys.

She grew silent as they sat chattering around the fire, vying with each other in saying witty nothings. Soon darkness began to creep down from the woods and shut them into a circle of firelight. Someone called for a story. As usual on such occasions, no one could think of a story—that is, no one but Lona. She had not listened to Pappy Hall's yarns for nothing. "I kin tell you about Pete, the One-eyed Mule," she volunteered.

"Go ahead."—"Throw in the clutch."—"Put your foot on the starter," they urged.

"Wal, Pete was a mule that was the property of old Uncle Jim Pease, up in Coon Holler," she began, in almost exact imitation of Pappy's drawling tone. Quiet settled down upon the restless, whispering circle. It was broken only by an occasional chuckle. All glances were fixed on the bright-eyed face of

Lona, who was totally unconscious of them. She was far away back in her own mountains, listening to Pappy. Wider and wider grew the grins, as the tale progressed to its climax. An instant explosion of laughter came as Lona ended, "And that's why Uncle Jim never did git that corn to the mill."

"Another! Another!" they demanded. Lona saw that the glow of the fire had grown fainter and that the darkness was now thick and close about them. "Would you all like to hear about the time Pappy Hall saw a 'hant' up the branch?" The boys and girls huddled close to the fire and prepared to feel creepy. They considered ghost stories "baby stuff," but they felt that Lona's "hant" story would be different.

The mountain girl did not disappoint them. She believed that there was a "hant" up in the rhododendron thicket on the branch. She was certain that Pappy had seen it and heard it crashing through the woods, and for the time being, she made these young people feel as she did. Their eyes grew wide as they listened to Pappy's adventures. Lona's "hant" was more real than any flesh-and-blood person they had ever known.

Chapter 17

Lona Makes a Public Appearance

In spite of her success at the beach party, Lona remained a "funny little kid" to Janet and her friends. She felt shy and uncomfortable when she tried to join in their talk. Why, she did not know the meaning of many of the slang words they used, and they understood her talk little better. But the twins took her to their hearts when they found she could tell tales of moonshiners and shootings and "hants," scarcely letting an evening go by without begging for a story.

The top-floor workroom remained her favorite retreat. Here she felt nearer Hollybush than anywhere else. Here she was herself. She sang in time to her shuttle's plying, sang the old ballads and hymns of her mountains. One day Mrs. Gregory, on her way to the third floor, stopped in the middle of the stairs as she heard the girl's sweet voice singing:

> *"There was a silk merchant,*
> *In London he did dwell.*
> *He had one only daughter—*
> *The truth to you I'll tell,*
> *O, the truth to you I'll tell.*

> *"Her sweethearts they were plentiful,*
> *She courted both day and night,*
> *Till all on Jackie Frazier*
> *She placed her heart's delight,*
> *O, she placed her heart's delight."*

In verse after verse Lona told the old love story through to its "happy ever after" ending, while the cloth grew in her loom:

> *"And now they're happily married,*
> *In Germany they do dwell.*
> *This story to their children*
> *So often they do tell,*
> *O, so often they do tell."*

Mrs. Gregory came up the rest of the stairs on a run. "Lona," she announced, "you simply must sing some of those old songs at our next Tuesday Afternoon Club meeting. I'll dress you up in an old-fashioned dress, and you'll sit at a spinning wheel and at least pretend to spin as you sing. And after you've sung for a while, you'll tell the club ladies about your weaving and about your plans for Hollybush."

Lona's eyes and mouth opened wider and wider as Mrs. Gregory unfolded her plan. "But I can't sing good enough," she objected, "and they'll laugh at the way I talk."

"Laugh! Not a bit of it; they'll be delighted. You really mustn't say no, Lona, for it may mean future sales for your work."

Mrs. Gregory went to work enthusiastically to cut and baste some pink cotton material she had in the house and evolved from it an old-fashioned dress and sunbonnet. Meanwhile, Lona rehearsed the old ballads to her loom and practiced the little talk she was to give, wishing fervently that next Tuesday would never come.

"Isn't she quaint? Isn't she lovely?" the ladies exclaimed

with delight when they saw Lona sitting at her spinning wheel, looking like an old-fashioned picture, and listened to the centuries-old ballads she sang. Her audience clapped until they had heard all the song-ballads she knew and some of them twice over. Still they clapped. Finally, Lona sang Mammy Hall's favorite hymn, ending with the refrain that had so often rung through the old weaving cabin:

> *"All glory to Him I bring.*
> *With gladness to Him I cling.*
> *With perfect delight,*
> *By day and by night,*
> *This wonderful song I'll sing."*

Then Lona stood up, fixed her eyes on Mrs. Gregory as a friendly support to her courage, and began to tell about "Forty-nine Snowballs." She described the yellowed paper in the old tin box, the resurrection of Mammy's loom with Preacher Johnny's help, the dyes that came out of Aunt Betsy's old black kettle, the packing of the coverlet and sending it off in Bije's wagon, and her excitement when the ten-dollar prize money arrived.

"I don't guess I'd be here if I hadn't made money weaving," Lona confessed. "Those kivers made me enough money to pay my carfare and buy the material fer a new dress fer me and a doll carriage fer Gail. She didn't have nothing but an old box on wheels Preacher Johnny made." At this point, someone wanted to know who Gail and Preacher Johnny were. Before Lona had finished talking, those Arden ladies felt as though they almost knew the household on Wildcat Ridge and Mammy Hall, Preacher Johnny, and the other neighbors. They could see the thin-soiled hillsides along Hollybush Creek, the cows that never could find enough to eat on those rain-gullied slopes, the scrawny pigs that wandered along the creek

Then Lona ... began to tell about "Forty-nine Snowballs."

and through the woods. And they shared the mountain girl's eagerness to "do something about Hollybush folkses being so poor."

Lona thought she never would get a chance to stop talking and sit down again. Nearly everyone had some question to ask. The simplicity and directness of her talk had roused more interest than practiced eloquence could have stirred. Finally, the chairman called the group to order for a business meeting, and Lona slipped into a corner.

She wasn't paying much attention to the "I moves" and "All those in favors." Her thoughts were still in the mountains. Suddenly she heard the words "Hollybush Creek." What were they saying? "The motion has been made and seconded," said the chairman, "that we use a portion of our social-service fund to buy a new loom and weaving materials for Hollybush Creek." An ecstatic "Oh-h-h-h," escaped from Lona's lips before she could stop it. The motion was carried unanimously.

Back in her room at the Gregorys', Lona stood in front of the looking glass and studied the reflection of a girl in a pink dress and pink sunbonnet. Could they be true—those things she had overheard the ladies saying? Was she a beautiful girl? Did she have lovely eyes? She was sure she had heard aright, and they were talking about her—Lona Allen from Hollybush Creek!

Chapter 18

Goodbye to Arden

It was September. Lona was bent over her suitcase, folding and packing her small outfit of clothes. She was getting ready to start on the long trip back to Hollybush Creek. Strangely enough, she did not want to go. Such a little while before she had longed for home by day and dreamed of it by night. Now the time had come to return, and she wished she might stay away longer. She still yearned to see Sairy Ann and Dick and Gail and the others, but it made her sad to think that in her whole life she might never see the Gregorys again. To tell the whole truth, the mountain girl had become a little spoiled by the attention her unusual personality had won for her and by the comforts and pleasures of the level country.

"Wonder what it will seem like to be back on Hollybush," she thought, a little anxiously. "Reckon Mammy Hall's weaving cabin will look dark after weaving in that big room with the skylights. I don't guess I'll ever see the ocean again or go bathing in it, or ever have such wonderful rides."

Mr. Gregory and the twins went to the city and saw her off. "Don't forget that I'm coming down to look over your weaving business when you get it going," Mr. Gregory told her. "And we're coming too," said the boys. "And we'll ride around on

Whitey's back and see all the moonshiners and everything." They stood on the platform, the boys waving their short arms and Mr. Gregory swinging his hat, till the train carried her out of sight.

Not until she was many miles on her journey could Lona stop thinking about the Gregorys. Gradually Arden faded into the background of her mind, and her thoughts began to run on ahead of the train to Hollybush Creek. Would Gail remember her and rush into her arms the way she used to? Had she grown? What would Mammy Hall think of the new loom that was coming with her on this train? "Going home! Going home!" said the engine, as if it knew that she was on her way back to Wildcat Ridge, to Aunt Sairy and Uncle Dick.

As the train came into Blairstown the next day, Lona strained her eyes to see who was on the station platform. There was Bije, looking as though he had not moved since she went away, in his faded blue shirt and khaki trousers. Beyond Bije stood—yes, it was Uncle Dick—and at the sight of him, Lona could hardly keep from jumping out the window.

Jolting along up-creek in the mail wagon, it seemed as if she had never been away. Yet she was seeing Hollybush with new eyes, critical eyes that noticed how mean were the bare little cabins, how thin and tired were the women, and how rough was the creek road.

"Howdy, Lona," called Granny Slone from her gate. "What-all you got in behind there?"

"Howdy, Granny," called back Lona. "It's a loom."

"What you aimin' to do with another loom?"

"Weave on it."

This reply naturally did not satisfy the old lady, but the wagon was by now out of earshot.

At the foot of the ridge trail, a little group waited for the mail carrier's wagon—Sairy Ann, Gail, Mammy and Pappy Hall, Lije, Rachel, and Whitenose. "Lona, Lona," called a piping voice, and Gail fairly flew into the outstretched arms of her returning playmate. They went up the trail, a merry procession. Gail, perched on her father's shoulder, sang a little song of her own, "Lona's tum home, Lona's tum home, Lona's tum home." Lije almost drowned her out with:

> *"She'll be comin' round the mountain,*
> *When she comes."*

Whitenose, cuddled in her mistress's arms, purred loudly a welcome home of her own.

Lona looked up at the House with Many Windows perched on the hillside and decided that there never was a house anywhere in the world quite so pleasant. She sniffed appreciatively, as the fragrance of fried chicken was wafted down the slope. "Must be company coming," she said.

"There is," agreed Sairy Ann, "and it's you."

> *"There'll be chicken stew and dumplin's*
> *When she comes."*

sang Lije.

They were a happy family party at supper that night, feasting on chicken and trying to tell each other everything that had happened since June. "Lona Allen," said Dick finally, in warning tones, as she helped herself to a biscuit for the eighth time, "if you eat that, you're going to burst." But Lona took the dare and proceeded to butter and eat the flaky morsel. "Uncle Dick, if you hadn't had nary a biscuit all summer—nothing but light bread—you wouldn't care if you did burst."

Lights burned on the ridge long after Mammy and Pappy Hall had gone home and the cabins along the creek were all dark. Lona could not tell her summer's tale in an hour or two. Nor could Sairy Ann and Dick bring her up-to-date on Hollybush news without many stories both grave and happy. The most important announcement they saved for the end of the evening.

"How would you like, for a change, to spend your days weaving and your evenings studying?" asked Dick, looking as though he knew what the answer to his question was going to be. "Sairy Ann and I have been talking it over, and we are willing to help you with your studies here at home so that you can now make a regular business of weaving."

Lona's face literally glowed with happiness. "Then I won't have to be the backwardest girl in the Hollybush School anymore," she said, as though she could hardly believe it to be true.

Chapter 19

New Furniture in the Old Cabin

Lona woke the next morning to find the house silent. Breakfast was long since eaten and cleared away. There was a great difference between the rising hours of Hollybush and of Arden. On the table was a note from Sairy, saying that she and Gail had gone to the store and to see Aunt Sally. Dick was out on a round of visits to the sick, and Lije was off on one of his aimless wanderings.

With a lost feeling, Lona ate her breakfast and washed the dishes. How lonely it seemed! There was not a sound to be heard except the murmur of Hollybush Creek and a rooster crowing. She stood on the porch and looked down at the stony creek road and at Granny Slone's and Preacher Johnny's weather-beaten cabins and grassless dooryards. Would she ever again ride in a soft-cushioned, joltless car over a smooth road? Or go to a palace-like theater? In spite of her joy over seeing her family, Hollybush seemed a drab and dreary place.

A restlessness laid hold of her such as she had never felt before. She started up through the young orchard Sairy Ann and Dick had planted and climbed on through masses of goldenrod and a thicket of laurel to the beech woods on the top of the ridge. Having reached the top, she started down again, too restless even to sit on the flat rock and enjoy the view. "I'll go up to Mammy Hall's and see how the new loom looks," she decided. Pappy Hall and Preacher Johnny had set it up in the weaving cabin the night before.

"Child, it sure seems natural to see you here again," said Mammy as they stood in the cabin doorway. "But that new loom looks strange in this old place. What-all you got in that-there box?" She pointed to a large wooden box beside the loom.

"Enough linen thread to weave dozens of tablecloths, Mammy, and yarn and cotton warp for kivers." She told of the club meeting and how the loom and the box of materials were given to her and of the order for weaving she had brought back.

"I ought to go right to work this minute," said Lona, "but somehow, Mammy, I can't settle down and do anything."

"I recollect Sairy Ann used to act like a lost pup for the first few days after she done come back from the level country. You'll be feelin' to home by the end o' the week."

Lona tipped back in her chair and suddenly noticed two wrought-iron lanterns that hung from the smoke-blackened beams overhead.

"Where'd you git them?" she asked, pointing upward.

"Peter Gayheart, he made them out o' some old iron this summer when he was home and asked me if he could leave them. He took such a fancy to the place, I let him work in here. Handsome, ain't they? But you'd oughter see the things he made—dishes fitten fer the Queen o' England—or is it a King they's got there now?—and andirons and pretties carved out o' wood. And jest look at this here picture he made o' me outen clay." She pointed to an earthen plaque hanging on the wall that pictured her churning butter.

Lona hoped Mammy hadn't noticed how her cheeks had flushed at the mention of Peter. "Why, it's point-blank like you," she said.

"It makes me look right-smart better than I do," said Mammy, eyeing it doubtfully, "and my dress wasn't blue like that; it was black, but he thought blue would look prettier in the picture. Would you believe that folkses down in the level country buy that picture, and me a stranger to them?" It was evident that Mammy was pleased, though puzzled.

Lona decided she had heard enough about Peter and Peter's accomplishments. She began somewhat breathlessly to describe her summer at Arden, repeating much that Mammy had heard the night before. She whisked restlessly about the room, moving everything and attacking the summer's accumulation of dust so rashly and so vigorously that Mammy began to choke.

"Oh, child!" she exclaimed disgustedly, "what a to-do you are a-makin' round here."

"It's all in a mess," declared Lona peevishly, picking up a chair, moving it across the room, then putting it back in the exact spot where it had been. "Peter, he didn't take no care o' the place, and it ain't fitten to work in, nohow."

Mammy retired to the house, remarking that, "It warn't fitten to breathe in now."

When she had gone, Lona stood on a chair, reached up to the sooty rafters, took down the two lanterns and thrust them into the dimmest corner of the cupboard. "I don't want them up there, nohow," she said to herself, then added, as though some explanation were necessary, "They might fall down on my head." In her heart, she knew the real reason for banishing those lanterns. They reminded her of Peter, and she wanted to forget him. She shut the cabin door with a little bang and went wandering off up-creek. "I almost wish," she thought, "that I hadn't come back."

Chapter 20

Lona Aims to Help Hollybush

Lona unrolled from her loom a table runner woven in dull blue and pale yellow, held it off at arm's length, and pronounced it "nigh to being as fine-pretty as the 'Forty-nine Snowballs.'" Nothing she would ever weave, in her opinion, would reach the high-water mark of that first-prize coverlet with its rosy snowballs. She sat down in the sunlit doorway and began fringing the ends of the bright linen. So intent was she on her work and her thoughts, she did not hear footsteps. A shadow fell across the door-stone, and she looked up to see Mattie Boleyn standing there with her baby in her arms.

"Howdy, Mattie, come in and sit," said Lona. "How white and wore out Mattie looks," she was thinking. "Why, she's Aunt Sairy's age, and anybody'd guess she was years older." She looked down at the tiny morsel wrapped in a patched baby blanket that lay in Mattie's arms. "How's the baby?" she asked.

"Right-smart pert." Mattie looked wistfully at the folds of blue linen in Lona's lap and came straight to the point of her visit. "Do you reckon I could learn to weave?"

A little more than two years ago, Lona had asked that same question of Mammy Hall. Now it was her turn to pass on what she had learned. The thought gave her a feeling of having

*She looked up to see Mattie Boleyn standing
there, with her baby in her arms.*

grown up and become of importance. "I'll teach you what I knows," she offered.

"And—and kin I sell what I weave and make money, like you do?"

Lona sensed the desperate need back of the faltering question. It was in the anxious tone of Mattie's voice and in the frantic expression of her eyes. Looking into the pale, old-young face, Lona vowed to herself she would do everything in her power to help Mattie. "Maybe," she said, "Uncle Dick would buy another rag rug; that's what you'd better learn on, and when you gits to making kivers and things, we'll try and find somebody down in the level country to buy them."

The tense lines in Mattie's face relaxed. She leaned back in her chair and began to talk without restraint. "It's months since my man has had more'n two days' work a week over to the mines. If things goes on this way, I'll have to keep Jimmy and Sally Lou shut up in the house all winter. I ain't got nary a whole pair o' shoes fer either o' them."

"They'll have some shoes before it's cold weather," said Lona confidently. "Now let's find Mammy and ask her if you kin use her old loom. Reckon the chickens are roosting on it agin."

When Mattie went back down-creek that afternoon, the discouraged droop had straightened out of her shoulders, and her face looked years younger. Lona's confidence was contagious.

Sam Boleyn drove his mule up to Mammy Hall's that same evening, loaded the loom into his jolt wagon and went rattling down the creek road with it. Bright and early the next morning, Lona started for Mattie's cabin to give her first weaving lesson and to carry the good news that Uncle Dick was ready to buy two rag rugs and would pay ten dollars for them.

Two weeks later, Mattie rode up Wildcat Ridge with the two rugs tied to her saddle. She turned her head quickly as she took the two five-dollar bills from Dick's hand, so that he might not see the tears that came into her eyes—tears of relief and happiness. But Lona, standing in the clinic doorway, saw and made up her mind that Mattie should have more opportunities to make money.

"If you wants to come over to the cabin, I'll give you the yarn fer a kiver," she said. "Then, when you gits it dyed, let me know, and I'll ride Whitey over and help you put up your warp and start weaving it."

That afternoon Lona spent at an occupation she hated—writing letters. She wrote to Mrs. Gregory and to the other Arden ladies who had given her orders for weaving, to Mrs. Whipple, and to her friend who had bought the green-and-white coverlet. Her letters were brief—stating that she was ready to fill orders for hand-woven coverlets, rugs and table linen and asking each if she would pass the word along to her friends. "A heap more girls and boys can go to school," she wrote, "and Hollybush children can have more to eat if I can teach the mothers to weave and then sell what they weave. That is what I aim to do."

It was a long afternoon's work, even if the letters were short, for she wrote a penciled draft and showed it to Sairy Ann, then copied and re-copied each one, to make sure there was not a mistake or a blot.

Next morning, as Lona was weaving, Mary Caudle rode into the yard on a bony old mule with her three-year-old boy and her year-old baby on the saddle in front of her.

"If I made two rag rugs, do you reckon anybody'd pay me ten dollars for them?" she asked before she had even hitched her mule. "The cow, it died, and Mat, he ain't got any money to buy another, and the children don't have no milk."

Lona looked at the thin little legs projecting from the boy's faded blue overalls and at the white face of the baby; she did some hard thinking and did it quickly. She could not ask Uncle

Dick to buy more rugs. He needed all the money he could get to buy medicines and supplies for the clinic. Suddenly she remembered the blue luncheon set she had just sent to Mrs. Gregory and the check she would be getting in a few days. She had picked out a coat for herself in the mail-order catalog and was planning to send for it just as soon as the money came. It looked simply beautiful in the picture, with a big fur collar and handsome buttons. Oh, well, she could wear her old one a while longer, and those children had to have milk right away.

"Yes, Miz Caudle, I knows someone who would pay you ten dollars fer a pair o' rugs," said Lona quickly, afraid she might change her mind if she gave herself time to think about that coat. "Have you got a loom?"

"Aunt Sophy says I kin have her old loom if I'll fetch it outen the attic."

There was a happy smile on Mary's face when she said goodbye, but Lona looked grave. A long sigh escaped her lips as she watched her visitors ride through the gate. She could still see herself in the new coat with the soft fur collar about her neck. "The Lord loveth a cheerful giver," she said to herself firmly. Well, perhaps she could be cheerful tomorrow, but she couldn't be today—not till she had forgotten how that coat looked in the picture.

"Clackety-clack!" sounded from Lona's weaving cabin, where her shuttle went to and fro, as swiftly as a hummingbird on the wing, across a strip of yellow linen. "Clackety-clack!" was heard from sun-up till dusky-dark in the Boleyn kitchen, where Mattie wove feverishly on a "Lee's Surrender" coverlet, stopping only to feed her children and her man and to milk the cow. "Clackety-clack!" came from the Caudle cabin up the branch, where a colorful, striped blanket was growing on Mary's loom. Up in a lonely Coon Hollow cabin, another old loom clattered as Holly Reynolds wove a rug.

The cause of all this hurry and clatter was the annual

Christmas bazaar of the Arden Tuesday Afternoon Club. "Send me anything you can have ready before the tenth," Mrs. Gregory had written. "I can't promise that we shall sell everything, but you're sure of some sales, and it will help make new friends for you and your Hollybush weavers."

Lona worked in her cabin every minute of the daylight, except for time out to eat and the time she spent riding Whitey on visits to Mattie, Mary, and Holly. She was restless and discontented no longer. The pleasures of the level country were forgotten. She was having the most fun she had ever had in her sixteen and a half years.

Early on a Monday morning in December, three mules were headed for the weaving cabin. One came from lower Hollybush. One picked her way down the branch trail, which was hardly a trail at all, and the third trotted down the rough Coon Hollow trail. Across the three saddles were bulky packages, starting on the first stage of a long journey out of the mountains and up north.

"I jest made out to git it done," said Mary Caudle as she untied from her saddle the soft blanket she had woven.

"Oh, Mary," exclaimed Mammy Hall, who stood looking on, "you ain't gone done and worked on the Sabbath, has ye?"

"No, ma'am," said Mary innocently. "When the clock it said twelve Saturday night, I set it back to nine and worked till it said twelve agin."

Lona concealed her grins by bending over the baby and patting the cheeks that were much rounder and pinker than they had been two months before. "I'm sure glad I bought those rugs of Mary's," she thought, "but oh! I do hope Mrs. Gregory will sell my tablecloth so that I kin get that coat 'fore January."

That evening Lona sat at the table in her room with her head propped up on her hands and a history book in front of her. The only trouble was that she could not prop her eyes open. She must learn the list of presidents tonight, for Uncle Dick was going to give her a history test tomorrow night, and he would be sure to ask her to name them.

"Washington, Adams, Jefferson, Madison—" she began, then stopped, unable to go further. She started over again, "Washington, Adams, Jefferson, Madison—" Oh! Who did come after Madison? And what difference did it make who he was? He was dead. But Uncle Dick would think she ought to know. Her head nodded for an instant, but she forced her eyes open, consulted the history book, and finally got through the list as far as President Tyler. "Tyler—Tyler—Tyler," she repeated, in a vain effort to remember his successor. Slowly her arms relaxed and refused to act as props any longer. In a moment, the history book was pillowing the tired head of "the weavingest girl."

Chapter 21

Santa Claus Carries a Heavy Pack

There never was such a Christmas before on Wildcat Ridge, because never before was there such a Christmas present as Richard Lawrence Junior, who arrived on Christmas Eve, "jest in time," as Lona said, "to put in a Christmas stocking." Granny Slone declared he looked "point-blank like Doctor Dick." Sairy Ann and Lona thought so too. But Mammy Hall accepted this verdict grudgingly, maintaining that her oldest boy, John, looked just like him when he was a baby.

Gail was the most excited member of the family. She bubbled over with joy as she ran back and forth between the china baby doll Lona had given her that lay in a tiny basket beneath the Christmas tree and the live baby doll in the clothes basket by the fire. As for Lije, he stood by the baby like a watchdog, as proud as though he were the father. "Got a boy this time. Got a boy this time," he proclaimed over and over.

Mammy Hall and Lona managed to cook the Christmas dinner, in spite of the number of times they had to leave the kitchen to show off Richard Junior to visitors. "I declare," said Mammy, "I don't rightly know what I'm doin' noways; 'twill be a wonder if I ain't put sugar in the biscuits and salt instead o' sugar in the puddin.'"

"And I'll burn the chicken to a cinder yet," added Lona, turning a wing over in the frying pan just in the nick of time.

The cooks' fears were all groundless. The chicken was a beautiful golden brown, the biscuits were Mammy's best, and the simple pudding had plenty of sugar in it.

Lona wore a shining face all day, partly because of the presence of Dick Junior, and partly on account of her own success as Santa Claus. Her tablecloth and napkins, Mattie's coverlet, and Mary's blanket had all been sold at the Arden bazaar. Holly's rugs had been returned, but Holly did not know it. Lona had paid for them out of her own earnings, and they now reposed on the floor of her bedroom. Of course, this meant saying goodbye to the new coat until another winter, but somehow, Lona did not greatly care. It was fun to play Santa Claus and to know that Christmas was happier in three cabins because she had lightened the worries of the families who lived in them.

Down on lower Hollybush, Jimmie Boleyn capered about in stout new shoes, and Sally Lou defied the December winds in a snug knitted suit. Up the branch in the Caudle barn, Lona, the new cow, munched hay contentedly. She was a bony beast, well along in years, but she gave enough milk for the children. The Caudles were as proud of her as though she were a blue-ribbon heifer. Holly Reynolds, away up in Coon Hollow, baked a Christmas cake. To be sure, it would not have been called a cake in a level country, but it was sweet and there was an occasional raisin in it. The two little girls, for the first time in their brief lives, had Christmas "pretties"—a cheap little doll and a red rubber ball. They too had warm woolly suits. "Isn't it wonderful," thought Holly, "that I sold my rugs so quick?"

There were surprises for Lona too this Christmas—gifts from the level country. Mr. and Mrs. Gregory sent a flame-colored sweater that helped to make up for the fact that she would not have a new coat. From Janet and the twins came a box of chocolates—the first box of "store-bought" candy Lona had ever received.

"Seems like I never did taste anything so good before," she said to herself as she let a caramel melt in her mouth. "Don't guess angels in heaven git anything better."

> *"Peace to the earth*
> *Goodwill to men,"*

caroled Lona, but she sang softly, so as not to wake the baby.

Chapter 22

Accusations

Lona sat in the weaving cabin, writing, writing, writing. Full-blown roses waited by the doorstep to be picked. Wild strawberries—deep red and fragrant—lay in the grass behind the springhouse. In the treetops, cardinals whistled and thrushes sang. But she was blind and deaf to the invitation June was giving her to come out. Instead she was writing, in her stiff, painstaking hand, a letter to Mrs. Warren.

Dear Mrs. Warren,
I'm glad you writ me about the folk-crafts festival. I am sending you a box of things. A good many Hollybush folks will be pretty happy if they sell.

Lona's pen was busier than her shuttle nowadays. She had a table in a corner of the cabin where she wrote notes to everyone she heard of who could possibly help to sell the work of her weavers. Fortunately, letter writing was easier for her than it used to be, though her letters were still childish sounding and her grammar was often peculiar. She did not have to consult a dictionary so often now. The ink behaved better about blotting, too.

She finished the letter, sealed it, took a fresh sheet and dipped her pen to begin another. Then she drew a sigh as she thought, "What a heap of letter writing it takes jest to sell one kiver!" Folks in the level country were poor these days, it seemed. (Lona had supposed that they were all rich.) They wrote about "hard times." "Had their crops all failed?" she wondered. How she hoped there would be a big crop this year!

A deep wrinkle drew her dark brows together. Oh! If she could, if she only could sell that "Sun, Moon, and Stars" coverlet. Mattie had worked over it till she couldn't sleep at night for the aching of her arms and back. She had spent the money she hoped to get for it over and over in her imagination. And there was Holly's blanket and Mary's bureau scarf. Only three pieces had been sold since Christmas—and one of those was her own. She had used all her money to buy Holly's rugs and Mary's second blanket. She had covered the floors of her bedroom and the weaving cabin with rugs and had tucked the blanket away in her marriage chest, along with her first "Forty-nine Snowballs." But she couldn't play Santa Claus any longer; her money was gone. And there were others who wanted to learn to weave and needed the money just as badly as Mattie and Mary and Holly. She hated to refuse to help them, but what was the use in teaching any more people to weave?

She set her jaw determinedly, jabbed her pen into the ink bottle and began—

Dear Mrs. Whipple,

While Lona sat writing letters and wondering how she was going to keep her weaving business from collapsing, Granny Slone was visiting Mattie Boleyn. The old lady was on her way home from one of her news-gathering expeditions downcreek. Hearing the clackety-clack of the loom, she had stopped "to see what Mattie was at now."

"What you aimin' to do with the hundred dollars when you gits it?" inquired Granny, when she had admired the pattern and asked question after question about the "new-fangled" dyes, and where "she done got the stuff to make it outen," and "who was a-goin' to buy it anyhow?"

"The hundred dollars!" exclaimed Mattie, breaking her wool in her excitement. "Whoever heard of gittin' all that fer a kiver?"

"That's what they done paid Lona fer hers."

"Oh, no, Granny! She got forty dollars fer them kivers. She told me so."

Granny shook her head. "That's strange—mighty strange. I was plumb certain that 'Forty-nine Snowballs' kiver fetched her a hundred dollars." The difference between the two amounts was rather vague in the old lady's mind. She had never possessed even forty dollars at one time in her life.

Having accumulated considerable information, including what Sam was doing and where he had been going last evening when Granny saw him riding by, and how many teeth the baby had, the visitor took her leave and went shuffling along up-creek, wholly unconscious that she had started a pot of trouble brewing.

Mattie continued her weaving but made slow progress. She said to herself that Granny must have heard wrong about the money. Yet somehow she could not put the old lady's remarks out of her mind and kept arguing the matter back and forth with herself. What if it were true that Lona was cheating her and the others—cheating them out of more than half of what they were earning? It couldn't be true. Well, how did she know Lona wasn't the kind of girl who would do such a thing? What did she know about Lona? Only that Sairy Ann and Dick had found her in a cabin up on the branch and taken her home. Nobody knew who her folks were or where they came from. She thought back to the time when Lona had sold that first coverlet and seemed to remember hearing something about a hundred dollars. By the time Sam came in for dinner, Mattie had convinced herself that Granny was right.

"What do you think I heard this morning?" she asked indignantly, then proceeded to tell him what Granny had said.

Sam Boleyn was hot-blooded and never slow to anger. "I'll have her in jail fer this, I will," he exploded.

After dinner, Mattie saddled the mule and rode up-creek. Her first stop was at Aunt Betsy's cabin. After "howdy's" and "how be you's" had been exchanged, Mattie turned the talk to the subject of kivers. "You helped Lona make her 'Forty-nine Snowballs,' didn't you?" she asked.

"I done showed her how to dye the colors," said Aunt Betsy, with pride in her voice.

"You recollect what the woman in the level country paid her fer it?"

The herb-woman shook her head.

"Was it a hundred dollars?"

"Might o' been, might o' been," admitted Aunt Betsy. "I knows it was a sight o' money."

Like Granny Slone, Aunt Betsy had seen so little cash that almost any sum from five dollars up seemed to her "a sight o' money." Her herb medicines were generally paid for in pork or beans, and she exchanged at the store the few eggs her hens laid for such commodities as coffee and sugar. However, Mattie did not take this fact into consideration. Firmly convinced that "a sight o' money" was a hundred dollars, she rode on up Hollybush.

At the headwaters of Hollybush, she turned up the steep branch trail and rode till she came to Mary Caudle's cabin.

"I couldn't believe that noways o' Lona—not after she's been so good to me," declared Mary stoutly when Mattie voiced her suspicions. "Granny Slone's got a wagging tongue, and she's a foolish old woman. Lona don't take none of our money, 'cepten jest enough to pay fer sending things to the level country. She told me about that."

"But don't you recollect hearin' how she got a hundred dollars fer that kiver two years ago?"

Mary shook her head.

"Well, I do. I'd forgot, till Granny reminded me. Maybe Lona has been good to you, but maybe she's been a sight better to herself."

Suspicion is a more catching disease than measles or scarlet fever. When Mattie unhitched her mule, Mary had all the symptoms her visitor showed. Her cheeks were as flushed, and her eyes were as dark with anger.

On went Mattie to the end of the branch trail, then up through the deep woods and over the ridge to Coon Hollow. She drew rein at the Reynolds cabin. Holly regarded Sairy Ann and Dick as the "best folkses that ever lived." They had helped her man Dave out of numerous scrapes and had cured her baby of scarlet fever. Lona shared their halo. Holly was sure that Granny was "mistook." She would never believe anything like that about Lona—never. Yet, after Mattie had talked a while, even her confidence was a little shaken. Finally, not without misgivings, she consented to join Mary and Mattie and Sam the next morning at Lona's weaving cabin.

On the morrow, Lona's pen was busy again. She was writing to everyone she had heard of in the level country who might be interested in buying or helping to sell the products of Hollybush looms. Having sent off a batch of letters the day before to the Arden ladies, she was now beginning on a list of people Sairy Ann and Dick knew in Clayburgh. The more letters she wrote, the higher rose her spirits. Surely, out of all these folks, there must be some who wanted the beautiful things she had to sell, and would buy, even if crops were poor. And perhaps she would get enough orders to set more weavers to work.

She stopped to rest for a moment, went to the door, looked out into the warm sunshine, and listened to a thrush that was sending peals of music ringing through the woods above the cabin. "What a fine-pretty morning!" she said to herself.

"Chicken crowin' on Sourwood Mountain,
Hey ho diddle dum dee-ay!"

She began singing merrily but stopped in the middle of the stanza as a procession of four, headed by Sam Boleyn, came walking up the path.

"Howdy, everybody," she called gaily. "I'll fetch some o' Mammy's chairs out here in the sun."

"Don't get no chairs. We kin stand up to say what we has to say." Sam's tone was grim.

The merry smile faded from Lona's face. "They look," she thought, "like they was on their way to a funeral meeting." Why had Sam come with the others? Had something happened?

They stood facing her in a little half circle, a jury of four—Sam, Mattie, Mary and Holly. "We wants to know," began Sam bluntly, "why you ain't payin' Mattie and Mary and Holly what they earns."

Lona looked from one to another in blank amazement. "Not paying them what they earns! Why, I ain't sold nary a thing fer months."

"I don't know nothin' 'bout that," went on Sam, "but I knows you done sold a kiver fer Mattie last Christmas, and all she ever got fer it was thirty-nine dollars and some cents."

Lona stared at Sam, unable to believe that he was accusing her of cheating. "But Sam—you don't mean—you don't think—"

"Yes, I do think. I think there's been strange doings. Your kiver fetched a hundred dollars. Why didn't Mattie git a hundred dollars fer hers? We wants to know point-blank how much the furrin women paid you fer Mattie's kiver and Mary's blanket and the other things. We has a right to know."

If eyes could burn human flesh, Sam would have been blistered at that moment by Lona's. "I never got a hundred dollars fer no kiver, Sam Boleyn. Mattie and Mary and Holly has been paid every cent they done earned and more'n they earned. I kin prove it. I kin show you every letter the furrin women has writ to me."

She dashed into the cabin. Her small nose was tilted defiantly upward. Her mouth was set tightly in a thin line.

Sam looked worried. "The little spitfire! She's madder 'n a trapped woods cat," he muttered.

"I wish we hadn't come," said Holly.

"Ain't I glad I kept every one o' them letters, like Aunt Sairy told me to," thought Lona as she jerked open the table drawer and pulled out a pile of letters carefully tied together.

"There, Sam Boleyn, read that and that and that." She thrust letter after letter under his nose and pointed to the statements about prices. Sam's head dropped lower and lower as he read. When he had finished and had passed the letters on to Mattie, his gaze was fixed on the ground. He was too embarrassed to face the anger and scorn in Lona's eyes.

"We—we was mistook! We didn't know—" he began apologetically. But Lona did not give him time to finish.

"Now, I wants to tell you all something—something I didn't never aim to tell you, 'cause I didn't want to make you feel uncomfortable about keeping the money. The rugs Holly made last Christmas didn't sell, neither did Mary's second blanket. They was returned, and I've got them right in there"— she pointed toward the doorway—"and up in my room at home. I paid Holly and Mary outen the money I got fer the things I wove, and I done without the coat I'd picked out in the mail-order book so's they wouldn't have to do without the

"There, Sam Boleyn, read that and that and that."

things they needed. And this is the thanks I gits, and I wish now I'd boughten the coat."

At this point, Holly relieved her own pent-up feelings and relieved the situation for everybody else by bursting into tears, throwing her arms around Lona and sobbing out, "Oh, Lona, I knowed you was good, I knowed you was good. I jest lost my head."

"We-uns all lost our heads," said Sam, and Mattie and Mary murmured agreement. "Mattie hadn't ought to listened to no old woman's talk, nohow. I'm sorry there's been ructions 'twixt us, and I hopes," he added solemnly, "you'll fergit the hasty words that has been spoke here this morning."

"What old woman's talk did you listen to?" asked Lona.

Mattie explained.

Granny Slone! The thought that they had taken a gossiping old woman's chance remark as evidence that they were being cheated was almost more than Lona could bear. For a few moments, she did not trust herself to speak. Sam shifted uneasily from one foot to the other as he waited. Mattie and Mary watched Lona's face. Holly blew her nose and wiped her eyes.

"We'll jest fergit about this morning—all of us," finally agreed Lona.

"But I'm a-going to pay you back fer the rugs," said Holly.

"And I'll pay fer the blanket," chimed in Mary.

Lona shook her head. "No, I'm a-going to keep them, and I wants you to fergit what I told you, jest like I'm a-going to fergit what you all have said. I didn't aim to give that secret away, nohow, but I got so mad, it jest came out."

When they had ridden away on their mules, Lona shut up the cabin for the day, crossed the creek, and climbed to the top of Wildcat Ridge. It was one thing to say that she would forget the incident and another thing to do it. "They thought

I cheated! They thought I cheated!" she kept saying to herself bitterly as she plodded along through the woods, not caring where she went and scarcely knowing what she did. Having walked till she was too weary to go on, she crumpled up on a rock and sat staring into space. Dinnertime came and went. The sun edged nearer the ridgetop. Still Lona sat and looked down through Paw-Paw Gap, seeing nothing.

Sairy Ann had just put the baby to bed and was beginning to get supper when Lona came in, as silent and white-faced as a ghost.

"Are you sick?" asked Sairy, in genuine alarm at the change that had taken place in the girl since morning.

Lona shook her head. "Reckon I'm hungry. I plumb forgot to eat any dinner."

Sairy refrained from more questions. "Have a glass of milk, and you'll feel better," she advised.

Lona sipped milk in silence for a few moments. "Oh, Aunt Sairy!" she exploded suddenly, unable to keep her misery to herself any longer. "The most terrible thing has happened to me today that could happen to anybody."

"Heavens!" exclaimed Sairy Ann. "Are you sure about that?"

Lona told the story.

"I don't blame you for being upset," sympathized Sairy, "but at least they haven't burned your weaving cabin down yet, the way they did the clinic, and nobody has called you a murderer. That's what they called your Uncle Dick. It's worse to be accused of murder than of cheating, don't you think so?"

"Whoever called Uncle Dick a murderer?" asked Lona indignantly.

"Aunt Betsy did—a long time ago. She doctored Joe Slone's woman with her herb teas till poor Maria was just ready to die. Then she got scared and told Joe he'd better send for Dick.

Dick went up there in the worst sleet storm I ever saw, when it wasn't safe to ride up and down these ridges. The thanks he got was to be told that his medicine killed Maria."

"And Joe Slone believed that of Uncle Dick?" Lona's expression was one of utter amazement.

"He sure did."

Lona was thoughtful for a little. "Well," she said, "I reckon if Uncle Dick could keep on a-doctoring after that, I kin keep on with my weaving business."

Chapter 23

A Busy Day

*"I'm a-goin' to shine like a star
In the mornin',"*

sang Preacher Johnny as he sat in his cabin door, tying bunches of grass together. Lona could tell by the ring of his voice that the old man was in a happy mood. On her way down-creek, she reined in Whitey to ask, "What you a-doing with all that grass?"

For answer, the preacher went into his cabin and brought out a hearth broom he had made by cutting the dried grasses into even lengths and tying them around a slender hickory stick. "That's what I'm a-doin' with grass. Folkses down in the level country buys them, too. Peter Gayheart says they does. And look at this here!" He picked up a small footstool he had made by weaving strands of hickory bark and cutting hickory sticks for legs. "Peter says he kin sell that, too. And that-there's a toastin' fork." The slow-moving, mild old man was actually excited by the possibilities he was discovering to his trade. "If he kin sell all this stuff, I'm a-goin' to git Maria a new Sunday dress."

Lona looked sober as she rode on down the trail to Mattie Boleyn's. Peter had been at home for two weeks, but she had not seen him except once at a distance. Before he went away, they had talked over their work and their plans together. Now, all she knew about what he was doing she heard second-hand. And, apparently, he did not even care to know what she did. A long sigh escaped her lips. "Git up, Whitey!" she urged as she drew near Peter's homeplace, kicking with her heels so violently that the old mule jumped up in the air, broke into a run and did not slow down till she had passed the Gayheart cabin.

"Howdy, Mattie," called Lona as she hitched Whitey to the board fence that kept wandering pigs from rooting in the Boleyn's neat yard. Mattie stood on the porch with the half-anxious, half-expectant look she always wore when Lona came to see her.

"I've sold your kiver," announced Lona, and stood still to watch a smile smooth out the lines in the tired face. "How good I am," she thought, "that I didn't have to disappoint her again. Mattie has been waiting fer that money ever since June."

"Reckon Jimmy kin stay in school all winter now," said Mattie. She gave a long sigh of relief, as though she were casting off a burden of worries. "I'll git him a coat and some rubber boots, so's he kin ford the creek."

"Arden folks are going to have that Christmas bazaar agin this year," said Lona, "and it ain't any too early to begin weaving fer it. How'd you like to make a 'Double Chariot Wheels' kiver? I've got the draft. 'Twould be pretty in dark blue and red; don't you think so?"

It was hard to get away from Mattie's. Sally Lou cuddled up in Lona's lap and kept saying, "Don't go yet," whenever she started to put her down. "Stay and eat dinner with us," Mattie begged her. "There's plenty o' beans and fatback." She was eager to make up for the unpleasant scene she had caused the week before.

"I can't stay, nohow," Lona had to explain over and over. "I've got to go clear up to Coon Hollow and see Holly 'fore dinnertime, and you know how slow Whitey is."

It was well that Lona had allowed plenty of time for her ride to Coon Hollow. Granny Slone hailed her, and she had to answer a dozen questions before she could break away. Mary Hayes was waiting at her gate to ask, "Do you know how I could git me a loom, so's I could learn to weave? Me and Tim aims to git married in the spring, and we wants to build us a house down on that strip o' bottom land o' Pappy's yonder." She pointed up-creek around the bend in the trail to where the valley widened and left a strip of level land just wide enough for a cabin and a corn patch.

"Reckon we kin find one," said Lona. "There's still some o' the old looms that ain't been cut up fer firewood."

"Hope I kin sell what she weaves," thought Lona, a little desperately, as she and Whitey went on their way. "I'd sure like fer her and Tim to have a nice little house and some fine-pretty things in it."

"Whoa, Whitey!" Lizzie Gayheart, Peter's sister-in-law, was beckoning from her doorway. "Come in and see what Mark done made," she called as Lona threw the bridle rein over the gatepost. "I don't know what they're fer, but they's pretty, ain't they?" she asked, holding up for inspection a pair of bookends in the shape of squirrels. "And look yonder at them fire tongs and andirons. They's made outen old wagon-wheel rims and scraps of iron. Peter says somebody'll buy them fer Christmas presents, like as not." Lizzie looked as though she did not know whether to take such an idea seriously or to laugh at it.

Lona nodded reassuringly. "Most likely they will."

Holly's cabin was a sorry place compared to Mattie's and Lizzie's cottages. Her man, Dave, had been in jail for nearly a year—ever since a "revenooer" had dropped in unexpectedly one morning to see a moonshine still back in the woods that Dave was rashly operating in broad daylight. Pappy Hall had once prophesied that if Holly married her cousin Dave, she would always be in hot water, and his words had come true.

That was why Lona had paid for Holly's unsold rugs out of her own meager earnings. That was why she rode up to Coon Hollow as often as she possibly could.

Lona gave a little exclamation of delight as she entered the weather-beaten old cabin. At the two small windows hung homespun curtains the color of sunshine.

"You like them?" asked Holly. "Long as I wasn't making nothing to sell, I figured I might as well weave me some curtains like the ones you made fer your cabin."

When Lona had admired the curtains and watched Holly's youngest demonstrate that she could walk without tumbling down, she unwrapped her bundle of warp and yarn. "How'd you like to weave some bags? Mrs. Gregory says she thinks little things will sell better than big ones this year. I'll help you thread the loom up now if you want me to."

Lona had hoped to be home for dinner, but there was no refusing Holly's pressing offer to share her beans and cornbread and sour milk. It was midafternoon before she was starting back. Rounding the corner where the steep branch trail joins the Hollybush trail, she came face to face with Peter Gayheart, who was riding in the opposite direction.

"Howdy, Lona."

"Howdy, Peter."

Whitey stopped dead in her tracks and reached her long neck for a spear of grass. Lona yanked at the reins, but she might as well have tried to pull a tree up by the roots. She grinned. Peter grinned back. The coolness in the atmosphere seemed to melt.

"I reckon Whitey knows best," he said. "It's time you and I got together again."

Lona's smile was sufficient answer.

"I've been hearing about your weaving business," he told her, "and I'm proud of you."

"And I've been a-hearing wonderful things about you."

"We're going to do wonderful things—both of us. Let's talk everything over in the old weaving cabin again," he suggested.

"I'd like fine to show you my new loom," she said. The sparkling light Peter remembered was in her eyes.

"Tomorrow morning?"

Lona nodded.

With a wave of his hand, Peter was off toward the headwaters of Hollybush. Lona rode on down-creek, singing gaily, while Whitey put back first one long ear and then the other to listen.

Chapter 24

"You've Grown Up"

Lona reached into the cupboard, pulled out two wrought-iron lanterns and hung them from the rafters, then went to her loom and began to weave. Suddenly she laid down her shuttle, stepped to the door, and listened.

*"Good morning, good morning, good morning to thee,
And where are you going, my pretty lady?"*

There was only one person who sang the old song just like that. Lona stood and watched the tall figure coming up the path. Peter gave her a long look that began with the dark curls on her forehead, continued down her small, pink-gingham-clad figure to her white sneakers. "I haven't had a good look at you before," he said. "You're not the little girl I left here in this cabin two years ago. You've grown up." His gaze came back to her eyes and rested there. "Yet, somehow, you are the same Lona, too."

She was silent for a moment, while her dark eyes looked searchingly into his gray ones. "And you are grown up too, but not right-smart different," she decided.

They went into the cabin so that Peter could see the new loom, then sat down on the doorstep and talked. They drank the cool water in the springhouse from Mammy's cracked old gourd, sat on the milk-pan shelf and talked some more. Did two people ever have so much to tell each other? Finally, Mammy called in warning tones that it was long past dinner time and that they'd better come and have something to eat "'fore she done cleared it away."

She reheated the fatback and cornbread, picked wild raspberries for their dessert, and poured glasses of buttermilk, cool from standing in the springhouse. "Ain't they ever goin' to git done talkin'?" Mammy wondered. "They're the talkingest pair I ever did see."

Not till the sun was halfway down on its way to Wildcat Ridge did Peter remember that his mother had asked him to do an errand at the store. "Hope she didn't aim to use that sorghum for dinner," he said as Lona walked with him to the gate. "I almost forgot something else," he added, putting his hand into his pocket and pulling out a flat object. "I've sold more of these than any other plaque I've made, and I thought you'd like to have one. It's a little late for your seventeenth birthday, but we might call it a birthday present."

Lona gave a little gasp of surprise as she looked at a picture of herself bent over the heavy old loom. It was an earthen plaque Peter had modeled in clay and glazed in colors, and it was Lona to the life—dark, short curls, straight little nose, firm mouth, small, busy hands, red sweater. Across the bottom was inscribed, "The Weavingest Girl."

"I jest love it, but as Mammy Hall said about her picture, 'It makes me look right-smart better than I do.'"

Peter looked at his model and smiled. "It couldn't," he decided. Thereupon Lona's cheeks turned as pink as her dress.

And now remorse pricked her. This birthday gift reminded her of the little wooden cat Peter had given her on another birthday and of how she had thrown it in the fire. "There's something I did I'd ought to tell you about—something terrible," she began.

At the sight of her troubled face, Peter stopped in the midst of untying his mule and waited anxiously for what was coming.

"You recollect that-there little wooden cat you gave me three years ago on my birthday?"

Peter nodded.

"Well—I—I was so mad 'cause you didn't pay no heed to me that Christmas time, when you was home, I done went and—and burned it up."

"So you were mad because I let you alone, and I was mad because you didn't answer my letters."

At his mentioning the unanswered letters, a distressed look came into Lona's face. "Oh, Peter," she explained, "I tried over and over, and I couldn't write a letter fitten to send to a boy that has got all the book-learnin' you has. So I tore every one o' them up."

Peter threw back his head and laughed. "What silly children we both were! I'll make you a new wooden cat."

The loom in the cabin was idle the rest of the afternoon while Lona sat looking dreamily at nothing and thinking. She had told Peter that he was not "right-smart different." Yet he was different, she decided. He was more grown-up, more dignified, and there seemed a little distance between them, no matter how much they laughed and talked. She felt shy with this handsome young man who had taken her old friend's place. Yet some of the time he was the old Peter, especially when he smiled. It was the same gradual smile she remembered so well, beginning with a tiny twinkle in his eyes, then crinkling up the skin around them, and finally bombarding his firm, sober mouth and just making it turn up at the corners. Did he like her as much as he had seemed to once, she wondered.

They had talked mostly about their work, and he had given her new courage, just as he used to. Somehow, he had always been able to make the obstacles in her path seem trifling and to paint the skies ahead a rosy color. He was so sure she could do the things she wanted to do. There was a shop, he had said, out on the edge of the mountains, that would take her work and sell it for a commission. People came riding by that shop on the long, wide road that ran from far north to the tip of Florida. It would take time to build up her business, but she could do it, he was certain. Then he had said something about money the state might pay her. He was going to try to get them to pay him for teaching the boys and girls to do the things he knew how to do. If he succeeded, perhaps they would pay her for teaching the women and girls to weave.

Mammy Hall came out to the cabin and stood for a moment in the doorway, hoping Lona would tell her what she and Peter had found to talk about all that time. But the girl did not see her or hear her step on the door-stone. So Mammy tiptoed back to the house.

It was nearly dusky-dark when Lona finally roused herself from her waking dreams, shut up the cabin, and started for home. Granny Slone sat in her doorway, waiting to hail her as she passed.

"Peter, he's grown handsome since he went away, ain't he?" she called out.

"I reckon," agreed Lona noncommittally.

"I reckon that gal o' his down in the level country thinks so too," volunteered Granny. "Bije says he gits a sight o' mail, and Jim was a-tellin' how he's up to the store first thing after mail time most every day. There's jest one thing makes a young feller chase to the post office, and that's a letter he's 'spectin' from a gal." The old lady's cackling laugh followed Lona as she hurried up the ridge.

Chapter 25

Two on a Hilltop

"Do you ever do anything except work?"

"Not much, nowadays," admitted Lona.

It was one of those fall mornings when the world seems to be all of blue and gold—blue skies, blue haze on the hills, gold-colored foliage and mellow, golden sunshine. Lona was on her way to the weaving cabin. Peter, on muleback, had overtaken her and had reined his mule directly across her path.

"What you s'pose I have in there?" he asked, pointing to a bulging saddlebag.

"Something you made?" asked Lona.

Peter shook his head. "Something my mammy made—ham and light bread, a bottle of buttermilk, and some cake. I'm a-going over on Breakneck and fetch home some butternuts and maybe shoot a rabbit and eat my dinner up there and forget there's any such thing as work in the world."

"I never heard of anybody getting to Breakneck by going this-a-way." Lona waved her arm in the direction of the weaving cabin.

Peter grinned. "But I'm not going this-a-way," he mimicked her. "I'm going that-a-way. I came up here to get you to go that-a-way with me. We've both worked and worked and worked all summer and talked about nothing but work. It's time we went a-pleasuring together."

Lona laughed delightedly. "I haven't been picnicking in the longest time—seems like years."

They rode down the trail on Peter's mule, stopping to tell Sairy Ann where they were going and at the same time adding to their lunch some juicy apples from the thriving young orchard on the ridge.

Arrived on top of Breakneck, they hitched Abe, the mule, to a tree, took their baskets, and set out for the butternut trees on the farther slope of the mountain. The squirrels that chased about trying to salvage as much of their winter food as possible from the trespassers on their nutting grounds were no more frisky than Lona and Peter. They raced to see which basket should be filled first. They played catch with the nuts. They set a nut on a rock as a target and took turns trying to knock it off. They cracked out meats from the hard shells and ate them.

At noon, with well-filled baskets, they climbed back to the hilltop, put a feed bag on the braying mule, and sat down upon a carpet of beech leaves to eat their lunch. Something must have happened to the sandwiches and cake and buttermilk since Peter had stowed them away in the depths of his saddlebags that morning. Mere everyday food could never have tasted the way that lunch did to the two young people on the hill. Perhaps the indescribable tang of an autumn day gave it a rare flavor. Or it may have been that the merry chatter accompanying every bite acted as a spicy sauce.

"I thought Mammy was giving us too much," said Peter, as they finished the last crumb of cake and topped off with butternut meats. "I've eaten twice as much as I do at home."

"I haven't eaten like this since Christmas dinner," declared Lona.

They loafed under the beech trees.

They loafed under the beech trees, content to say little and to look much at the view spread out below them and the blue haze that filled the gap in the hills.

"I've seen pictures of a lot of furrin places," Peter mused out loud, "but I don't recollect that I ever saw any picture as pretty as this one."

Lona looked down through the woods to where the creek was a narrow brown ribbon, and the cabins nestled in the hollows of the hillside beyond looked like dollhouses at that distance. She nodded complete agreement. "I've seen China and India and—and—Brazil and France and a heap o' places in the movies, but they don't look so good as hereabouts, noways."

They wandered along the high ridge together, scuffling in the leaves, climbing up the sloping side of a great rock to jump off the steep side, chattering gaily. It was late afternoon before they poured their baskets of nuts into the saddlebags, untied the stamping mule, and headed him homeward.

Peter, as if he hated to have the excursion come to an end, encouraged Abe to amble along at his slowest walk. When they reached the Gayheart cabin on lower Hollybush, he let the mule stop at the gate. "Got something I want to show you," he explained, as he helped her down, "a dish I just got fired. It's the prettiest I've ever done."

He brought out from a dusty corner of his barn workshop a bowl that made Lona give a prolonged "Oh-h-h" of admiration. It was beautifully shaped. On the outside, the glaze was a soft gray; within, it shaded from seashell pink to tints of rose, and the glaze lapped over the edge irregularly upon the gray like the petals of a flower.

"You said once when I showed you my prize kiver that I was an artist," Lona reminded Peter. "Well, that's what you are, point-blank."

They sat on the porch with Mammy Gayheart and drank the fresh milk she poured foaming from her milking pail, then, as it began to grow dusky-dark, went on to Wildcat Ridge.

"Howdy," called Granny Slone, peering out of her door to see who was going by. "Where you two been all day?"

"Picnicking," Lona called back gaily.

"Picnicking, humph!" muttered Granny to herself. "Them two is a-sweetheartin', and that Peter Gayheart is a-triflin' with Lona's affections fer certain. Once a boy's been to the level country, he ain't satisfied with no mountain gal fer his woman, not noways." She shook her head gloomily.

Chapter 26

Lije Is Forgetful

"I hope he never comes back—never, never, never," said Lona to herself as she slammed her feet down on the treadles and jabbed her shuttle through the warp.

Peter had gone off to Clayburgh without telling her he was going or even saying goodbye. Granny Slone had just passed the news on to her that morning. "He got a letter day 'fore yesterday marked 'special delivery,'" Granny had told her. "Jim says that means it's in a swivvet. And Peter, he rid down to Blairstown with Bije yesterday and done took the train. I asked his mammy what he'd gone fer, and she said it was some business o' his. I reckon it's the business o' gettin' married. Bije tells me he was all dressed up in his best suit o' clothes and new shoes."

Lona scarcely knew what she was doing as she sat in the cabin trying to weave, saying over and over to herself, "I hope he never comes back." If only he had stayed down there and not come home at all! She had forgotten how much those talks they used to have together meant to her, forgotten how his friendship made living more fun. Then he had come singing up the path again, smiled that rare smile of his, and given her "the Weavingest Girl." He had showed her bits of his work and admired her weaving and encouraged her. They had made great plans together. Why, they'd been almost like partners. And now he had gone off without a word. Granny was probably right about the reason for the trip. If it had been business, he certainly would have told her about it. After she had broken her thread four times, Lona decided to quit weaving and go and help Mary Hayes put up her warp.

"Have you seen the pretty dishes and things Peter Gayheart is a-making?" was one of the first questions Mary asked her.

Lona nodded with apparent lack of interest, but Mary was not discouraged from talking about Peter. "He's going to learn me to make dishes to set up housekeeping with. Lizzie, she's making a fine-pretty tea set, and he says he kin sell it fer her."

"Looks like he's coming back," thought Lona.

The rest of that week she worked as though a whip was over her back. When she was not clattering away at her loom, she was riding up or down the creek on some errand, vainly trying to keep so busy she would have no time to think.

On Saturday morning, nearly a week after Peter's sudden leave-taking, Lona started for the store to do some errands for Sairy Ann. Behind her a familiar voice sang:

"Good morning, good morning, good morning to thee."

She walked on without looking around. The singing stopped, and a voice called gaily, "What's your hurry, Lona?" She turned to see Peter taking long steps to catch up with her. He was the picture of jubilance. The long lock of brown hair on his forehead stood up in the breeze like a bright pennant. His eyes did not twinkle; they sparkled. He seemed scarcely to touch the earth as he covered the space between them.

"I just got back last night," he announced, "and I could

hardly wait till morning to tell you everything. I've got good news."

Lona waited, unable to think of anything to say.

"She looks," thought Peter, "as solemn as if I had told her somebody was dead."

"Congratulate me," he said, holding out his hand. "It's all settled."

"Congratulations," said Lona, putting a limp hand into his and returning the warm, strong pressure of his hand not at all.

All of the sparkle went out of Peter's eyes. "You don't seem the least bit glad, and I thought you'd be almost as happy as I am."

"Of course, I'm happy about it." The words came out jerkily, and her voice sounded strange, even to herself.

"Well," said Peter, and now his voice too was jerky and strange-sounding, "I reckon I'd better get back to my work." Without another word, he turned and walked quickly downcreek again. As he walked, he fingered the new wooden cat that lay in his pocket. "I'll never give it to her now," he decided.

"So he took all that trip jest to git hisself engaged," thought Lona. Well, things would never be the same between them again. She must make up her mind to that.

"Do you reckon I could git me a job if I went back to Arden?" asked Lona as she helped Sairy Ann prepare dinner.

"Do you really want to go back there and leave us and Hollybush and this work you are just getting started?"

Lona nodded, feeling that she was being "weighed in the balance" and "found wanting."

"Well, I sure am disappointed in you. I'd no idea you were such a quitter, Lona. You've got a chance to do a great deal to help folks here, and you get sick of it before you've hardly begun and want to go where you can have a good time. It doesn't seem a bit like you."

"'Tain't a good time I want," protested Lona.

Sairy saw misery in Lona's face and grew sympathetic. "What's wrong now? Has somebody told you cheated again?"

"Nothing much," said Lona, and she would say no more.

A feeling of utter loneliness took possession of her. To no one, not even to her Aunt Sairy or to Mammy Hall, did she feel like telling what was on her mind.

> *"My true love, she lives in Letcher,*
> *Hey ho diddle dum dee-ay.*
> *She won't come and I won't fetch her,*
> *Hey ho diddle dum dee-ay."*

Lije sang at the top of his voice as he took his loose-jointed way up-creek. He was off for a morning in the woods rabbit-hunting. Lona, coming from the post office, interrupted his song and his progress. "Oh, Lije, don't you want to fetch this letter to Aunt Sairy? I've got something in my loom I aims to finish 'fore dinnertime."

At the sight of the letter, a conscience-stricken look came into Lije's childlike face. "I've got a little letter fer you. I done forgot about it."

"Where did you git it?" asked Lona.

Lije grinned. "Peter Gayheart, he give it to me."

Lona gave a start, and Lije's grin grew wider. She began to wonder if this were not one of the boy's fancies. He was always making up romantic tales about people. "Lije, when did Peter ever give you a letter fer me?"

"Might o' been last week, might o' been week 'fore that; I don't recollect." Time meant little to the slow-witted boy. He fumbled in the pockets of his overalls, pulling out nails, string, cartridges, pictures, bits of bright paper, but no letter.

Lona looked on, not knowing whether to take him seriously or to pay no attention to his talk.

"Reckon it's home in my pants," Lije decided.

She fixed him with a glance that compelled Lije to look into her eyes. "Tell me the truth. Did Peter give you a letter fer me?"

"He sure did. Leastways, 'twas a paper all folded up."

"Then we're both a-going home, and you're a-going to look till you finds it."

"I was a-goin' to ketch me some rabbits," protested Lije.

"You kin ketch rabbits after you've found that note," said Lona firmly.

The boy looked anxious as he tried to keep up with Lona's breakneck pace on the way home. "Hope I ain't done lost it," he worried.

Lona waited while Lije searched his loft room and the pockets of the few articles of clothing he possessed. At last he swung himself down, holding in his hand a dirty, rumpled, folded sheet of paper.

"She won't come and I won't fetch her," he sang as he shouldered his gun and started out again.

Lona went to her room where she could be alone, and then she opened the note.

Dear Lona,

I got the letter I've been expecting for weeks from the State Department of Education, and I'm off for Clayburgh this afternoon. I think I'm going to get an appointment to teach manual arts in this county. That will mean a lot to my work. Wish me luck. Sorry I can't see you again before I go.

Your friend,
Peter

Lije was only halfway down the ridge path when Lona passed him. "What's she in such a swivvet fer?" he muttered, for haste was something he could never understand. Open-mouthed, he watched as she hurried down-creek. "Where's she a-goin' to now?" he asked of the air.

Lona continued to be "in a swivvet" till she came within sight of Peter's home. Then she slowed down and strolled up the path, trying to act as though she just happened to be going that way. Mammy Gayheart called out a cordial "Howdy" from the porch and invited her to "come and set." They exchanged remarks about the weather, then Lona inquired casually if Peter were at home. "I've got a note here I sorter wanted to show him," she added.

"Pee-ee-ter," called Mammy. "He's workin' in the barn; that's where he keeps himself most all the time."

At Mammy's call, Peter's head was poked inquiringly out of the door. "Lona Allen's here to see you," Mammy informed him.

He came across the yard slowly, holding in his hand the piece of clay he was modeling, and greeted her, unsmilingly, in a well-what-can-I-do-for-you tone of voice.

Lona held out the abused-looking note. "Lije jest gave me this. He done forgot all about it. I can't half tell you how glad I am about the job, nohow. If I acted funny the other day, 'twas cause I didn't know what you was talking about. And—and I was all upset over something that morning."

Mammy Gayheart wisely withdrew into the cabin. To Lona's amazement, Peter turned without saying a word and started for the barn. She was just on the point of leaving when he called, "Wait a minute."

He was back in a moment, holding something small in the palm of his hand, and now even his mouth was smiling. "I made you a new wooden cat," he explained, handing it to her. "Let's call it our mascot, and let's not ever have any more misunderstandings about letters—or anything else, for that matter."

If you'll promise not to get mad at me and burn this cat, I'll promise not to jump at any more wrong conclusions about you or send any more important messages by Lije."

They shook hands solemnly over their pledge, then sat down and laughed till echoes rang merrily across the creek. When Lona went home, Peter walked all the way with her.

> *"With perfect delight*
> *By day and by night,*
> *This wonderful song I'll sing."*

The words of the old hymn floated from the cabin that afternoon to where Mammy Hall sat sewing. "She's singin' the way she used to," said Mammy to herself. "Something's made her feel mighty good."

Chapter 27

A Firm Is Incorporated

"Anything the matter, Peter?" Lona finally asked.

Peter had hardly spoken since he came in. He couldn't seem to sit still but kept walking up and down the weaving cabin. Now he was standing in the doorway, looking out, yet he did not seem to be seeing anything—just staring into space.

"What did you say?" he asked, turning around quickly.

"I asked what's the matter with you today."

"Er—nothing—nothing. I brought a little thing to show you." He made no move to produce the "little thing."

"Something you made?" asked Lona, thinking she had never seen him act so strange, so "like he had a scare on."

"Yes. I—I hope you are going to like it." He plunged his hand quickly into his pocket, jerked out a small linoleum block and held it out to her.

Lona studied the design cut into the block. At the top was pictured a tiny loom, at the bottom, a carpenter's bench. Across the center, in artistic lettering, were the words: "The Allen-Gayheart Industries."

"I wondered if—if—we couldn't go into a sort of—er—partnership and use that for a label," Peter explained, still embarrassed and hesitant. "We ought to have a trademark, don't you think?"

Lona of Hollybush Creek

"Why, that's a wonderful plan, Peter," said Lona. "'The Allen-Gayheart Industries': it's a fine-sounding name. I'd be right proud to use it fer a label. We'll be in business together now, won't we?"

"Why," thought Lona, "can't Peter act like himself?" He was blushing and running his fingers through his hair and walking up and down the floor again.

Now he was standing still and looking at her gravely. "I'd like to have another kind of partnership with you, Lona," he said quickly, as though he wanted to get the saying of it over as soon as possible. "I reckon you know what I mean. I reckon you know that I love you and want to marry you."

Lona looked as though she couldn't quite believe what her ears were hearing. "Seems like I'd always loved you, ever since I kin remember," she said, "and I knowed you liked me rightsmart. But I was afeerd you'd never want to marry a girl like me. I was afeerd you'd want a girl that was smarter and had more book-learnin.'"

Peter's laugh made the black old rafters ring. "I wouldn't care if you didn't have any more book-learnin' than Aunt Betsy or Granny. You're the smartest, prettiest, liveliest, nicest girl I ever saw, and I wouldn't change you any bit. I've been in love with you for years—ever since that time we danced the Virginia Reel at your birthday party, I reckon, though I didn't know it then. But I can see you now the way you looked that night."

What plans they made that November afternoon for the firm of Allen-Gayheart! How their eyes shone as they talked in front of a blazing fire in the cabin!

"Pappy says we can have the upper lot and a little piece down nearer the creek, and he'll help me get out the logs and build the cabin. It ought to be done come springtime if we start right away. I'll make a beautiful hand-carved mantel for the fireplace, and Preacher Johnny and I together can make all the furniture, and there'll be a best chair with carving all over the back, like one I saw in the level country."

Now it was Lona's turn to plan. "I've got my 'Forty-nine Snowballs' kiver and the blanket Mary wove and Holly's rugs. And I'll weave curtains for the windows—rose-colored curtains to match the snowballs in my kiver—and a tablecloth like the one I done wove fer Mrs. Gregory. Oh! I kin jest see the way it will look inside. We'll hang these lanterns"—she looked up at the wrought-iron lanterns Peter had made —"and you kin make some of these fancy andirons. It will be beautiful."

"There's another cabin I want to build; I've been thinking about it for a long time—years, I reckon," said Peter. "We could put it just above ours, in the upper lot."

Lona's eyes widened. "Another cabin? What would we do with another?"

"It wouldn't be for us. All Hollybush Creek would use this cabin. I can just see it. There would be two big rooms, with a chimney up through the middle and a fireplace in each room. One room would have looms in it and cupboards and chests for weaving materials. The women would come there to learn to weave and to dye their stuff. The other room would have carpenters' benches and a potter's wheel and all sorts of litter. And that's where I'd hold forth. Sometimes you will come in and say, 'Oh, Peter, what a sight this place is. Look how neat I keep my weaving room.' And I'll say, 'This is my side, and I can have it just as messy as I like.' But sometimes, maybe, I'll let you straighten it out a little, if you won't break any pottery."

He threw back his head and laughed merrily at his own fancies. Lona laughed too, out of sheer delight in Peter's plan.

"What's goin' on in here? A play-party?" asked Mammy Hall, looking in at the door. To Mammy's amazement, they both jumped up and threw their arms around her.

"Oh! Oh! Whatever is the matter with you two?"

They drew another chair up to the fire and made her sit

down while they told her their plans for the future. Mammy beamed. "I always hoped you two would git married, leastways, ever since I heerd you talk about each other, and I sorter knew you would someday."

"How you a-goin' to git you the money to build that-there workshop?" she asked, when Peter told her about the plan for the second cabin.

"Oh! I hadn't thought about that," exclaimed Lona.

"I had," said Peter confidently. "It's to be a neighborhood cabin owned by everyone who wants to use it. Some will give one log, some more than one. Others will give work. And one day, we'll have a working and invite everybody on the creek, and you and Lona and Sairy Ann will cook a grand dinner for them. And everybody who gives materials or helps will be a shareholder for life."

"And now," announced Lona, jumping up, "we are going home to tell Aunt Sairy and Uncle Dick. I can't wait any longer."

Sairy Ann forgot that she had a spoonful of egg yolk halfway to Richard Junior's mouth. In fact, she dropped the spoon in her excitement when Lona and Peter fairly fell upon her and told their news. The baby burst forth into a stream of unintelligible chatter, punctuated with gurgles and chortles. Whether he was delighted over the noise the spoon made clattering to the floor or over Lona and Peter's announcement, he did not choose to tell.

Gail stopped in the middle of putting her doll to bed to urge in tones of alarm, "Don't go away with Peter. Don't go away, Lona."

Lona kissed Gail's small mouth and helped her tuck the covers around the doll. "I'm not going yet, and when I do go, I'll be nearby and come to see you every day."

"I'm as happy about it as you are, I reckon," said Sairy as soon as she was given a chance to speak. "Only I feel like Gail about your going away, Lona. I hope we'll keep you here a little while longer."

"I can't begin to get things ready, nohow, till that Arden Christmas bazaar is over, and it's a-going to take a right-smart time to build the cabin and furnish it. Laurel time is a fine-pretty time fer a wedding, I reckon."

At this point, Lije, his face one broad smile, made himself heard. "I'll make ye a weddin' box," he announced. Whenever Lije heard that anyone was going to be married, he always presented the bride with what he called a "weddin' box" of his own design. It was a pasteboard box papered over inside and out with bright bits of paper, tinfoil, colored pictures—anything bright that Lije could find.

"I'd love to have a wedding box, Lije," said Lona. "I know it will be beautiful."

"Clippety-clop" sounded Twinkle's hoofs on the ridge trail. "It's Uncle Dick," cried Lona, running to the door. Before he had time to jump off Twinkle's back, she told him her news. Thereupon Dick picked her up as though she were the size of Gail, kissed her with emphasis, and set her down again. "That's the best news I've heard since Sairy Ann said she'd marry me," he declared.

"What's that you heerd?" Granny Slone was standing behind them. She had a special sixth sense that enabled her always to be on hand when there was news to be had. For the fourth time that afternoon, Lona told her plans.

"It's time you was gittin' you a man," said Granny. "'Pears like gals nowadays waited till they was old maids 'fore they done got married." Then, turning to Peter, "I was afeerd you'd go and git ye a furrin gal from the level country."

Chapter 28

Log by Log

Bud Hayes pointed up the steep slope beyond the withered stalks of his last summer corn to where two tall hickory trees stood out against the bare ridge. "You kin have them two trees yonder—cut and hauled. I been savin' them fer a new fence"—he looked a little regretfully at the sagging, rotting boards that enclosed his homeplace—"but they're yourn."

"I hates to take your fence," said Lona.

"You're welcome to it, you're welcome to it, after you been so good to my gal, teachin' her to weave. I kin give a day's work, too, when you gits ready to build the cabin."

Mary appeared in the cabin door. "I'd like right-smart to help. I'll weave ye some curtains fer the winders like them Holly wove, and I'm a-going to make me some fer my new cabin, too."

Lona was radiant. "That makes two shareholders in the neighborhood cabin in one family," she said and rode up-creek, well pleased with the way the morning had begun.

She was received with welcoming smiles at Uncle John and Aunt Sally's cabin, for the old couple were always happy to have company. "You take your hat and coat off and sit by the fire and stay and have dinner with us," urged Aunt Sally. "Now tell us when you and Peter are goin' to git married." The old lady settled down by the fire with a pan of beans to shell and made ready for a good visit. But Lona had to disappoint her; she had six more visits to make before dinnertime.

Uncle John scratched his head when Lona told her plans for a neighborhood workshop. "There ain't no trees left on my place, 'cepten them little popples up in the pasture that's hardly big enough fer a peckerwood to light on. Ifen I cuts them, that thar cornfield will all wash down into the creek. But you kin have all the stone you wants fer your chimbley, and I'll help ye build it, and a good one too. My pappy, he made this here chimbley ninety years ago, and there ain't a loose place in it today." He gave the chunks of limestone a resounding slap to show how firm they were.

"It will be splendid to have a chimney like that in the new cabin," said Lona, but she made up her mind that Uncle John's rheumatic old back and knotted hands would not be called upon to do any heavy work.

Lona's last visit that morning was to Preacher Johnny. She found him dreamily weaving strips of hickory bark across the seat of a chair. "I was jest a-thinkin' and a-wonderin' what I'd make ye fer a weddin' present," he told her. "It's got to be somethin' mighty fine, mighty fine, fer if you two ain't a-goin' to be the best-lookin' couple I ever married, then my old eyes is deceivin' me bad.

"And you're the prettiest gal—'cepten Sairy Ann. There won't never be another bride on this creek as pretty as she was. I kin see her now jest the way she looked that day she took the doctor fer her man. All in white she was, with a great bunch o' goldenrod and asters in her hands. It was September." The old man smiled at the recollection. Not even Lona, who was a great favorite of his, could ever quite measure up to Sairy Ann.

"I wish I'd been there to see her," said Lona. It was with difficulty that she brought the preacher back from his pleasant

"It's got to be somethin' mighty fine."

recollections to thoughts of the future and the cabin. "It will be a place where anybody kin work," she told him. "You kin bring your wood and grasses and things there, if you wants to."

"Reckon Maria would be glad to have me. I makes a heap o' litter sometimes."

Maria, who sat by the fire grimly plunging a churn dasher up and down in a churn full of cream, looked at the curls of bark and shavings on the cabin floor and expressed the opinion that "'twould save a sight o' sweepin.'"

Preacher Johnny sat in deep thought for so long a time that Lona decided he must have forgotten all about the cabin and was preparing his Sunday sermon. Finally, he voiced his thoughts. "You all are a-goin' to need another loom, ain't ye? I was thinkin' that mebbe I could make ye a loom point-blank like that thar one you brung home from the level country."

Lona jumped up and put her arms around the surprised old man's neck. "Preacher Johnny," she said, "that's exactly what I hoped you would do."

That afternoon Peter stopped at the weaving cabin to compare notes with Lona on the results of their morning's work. At sight of him, she waved a sheet of paper. "Eight logs, stone fer the chimney," she read from her list of promised contributions, "a loom (Preacher Johnny's going to make that), winder curtains, six workers, and they'll all give one day's work, anyhow. How's that? And I didn't even git to the head of Hollybush!"

"I knew you'd be good at this job," said Peter, giving her a kiss. "Your enthusiasms are as catching as measles."

Then he told the results of his own morning's work. "I went as far as the Bull Creek ford, and I didn't miss a cabin, not even old Pete Martin's, who thinks the neighborhood cabin will 'jest be a place fer the young folks to play-act and dance and have big times.'"

Lona laughed. "That's pretty nigh what Aunt Betsy told me."

"I can add five logs to your eight and ten workers," went on Peter. "I didn't ask for many logs; the ridge is bare enough down that way now."

Lona looked thoughtful. "I don't knows if I ought to take Bud Hayes' logs," she said. "He was aiming to build a new fence outen those trees, and he sure needs one."

"That's the worst of this plan of ours to have Hollybush build a cabin," said Peter. "Nobody has anything to give away that he doesn't need. But maybe folks will use the cabin all the more if they do sacrifice for it. Sometimes I feel like I ought to take the little money I've earned and buy the logs. But then we wouldn't have any money left to pay for our own cabin, and we mustn't postpone building that." He looked down into Lona's face and smiled a smile of pleasant anticipation. Her dark eyes reflected the light in his. "We've got to git it done by the time the laurel's in blossom," she said. "My mind is set on getting married then."

"We'll gather all the pinkest blossoms we can find," Peter told her. "You like them the best, and you'll be prettier than the prettiest bud that grows anywhere." He got up quickly. "And now, my mule and I, we are a-going way up the branch and then as far as the last cabin in Coon Holler. Up there's where the logs are."

"You won't find nobody up there interested in the cabin, I don't guess."

"I'll make them interested," vowed Peter as he jumped into the saddle.

"And he rode away, a-waving his sword," laughed Lona. "Well, I aim to dye yarn this afternoon, but tomorrow morning, I'll saddle Betsy and go over to Bull Creek and do or die over there."

Betsy was the new mule on Wildcat Ridge. Faithful Whitey, retired on a pension for several months, now reposed under an apple tree, with a handsome wooden marker above her.

Chapter 29

Such a Small Pile of Logs!

"Don't look like there'd be any neighborhood cabin up there next spring." Lona addressed this remark to a pathetically small pile of logs on the hillside as she rode by on Betsy. She said it again to herself as Betsy plunged into the chilly waters of the ford and started up the icy Bull Creek trail. "Those logs wouldn't build a cabin as big as Granny Slone's," she thought, "but I won't tell Peter that. Maybe we kin git enough to build him a cabin fer his pottery and carpentering and then next year add a weaving room."

It was December. Lona, wearing her old winter coat, was still riding the trails, visiting her weavers—who now numbered six—and talking, talking, talking about the proposed cabin to everyone within a radius of ten miles who had any growing timber. She was now on her way to the head of Bull Creek to see Joel Pease. He had plenty of wood growing in his ridge-top pasture, but so far she had not been able to extract from him the promise of the smallest stick.

Halfway up the trail, she overtook Joel, who was carrying a potato sack full of groceries. "I'll pack your poke up fer you," she offered. The old man gladly handed her the sack and walked along beside Betsy. "Was you a-comin' to talk to me 'bout that-there cabin agin?" he asked, on the defensive.

"Well," said Lona, "I was up this way, and I thought I'd prob'ly stop and see you and Miz Pease 'fore I went back, and of course I'm liable to talk about that cabin to anybody 'cause it's what I thinks about all the time nowadays." There was a twinkle in the girl's eyes.

"I ain't got no logs to give to make a place fer you young folks to have big times in," said Joel stubbornly.

Lona sighed. She had heard that objection so many times. "But we don't aim to have big times there. It's a place to work in."

By now they had reached Joel's cabin, and Cynthy was urging Lona to "come in and have a cheer." "This is where my mammy done all her weavin'—right in this here kitchen," announced Joel. "She done wove kivers and blankets and linsey-woolsey fer our clothes, and Cynthy and I is still sleepin' under them blankets and kivers. What's the matter with the gals nowadays doin' their weavin' ter home? They jest wants an excuse to git away from home."

Patiently Lona explained that the girls did their weaving at home but that they needed a place where they could come for their materials and where they could learn to weave new patterns and make dyes. "They can't learn from their mammies, like your mammy done learned. There's only a few old women that remembers how to weave. And none o' them kin weave on a new-fashioned loom like mine."

"If my mammy done all her weavin' in her kitchen, gals kin do the same today," Joel maintained.

Lona, realizing that they were right back where they had started, decided that she could not spend the entire morning arguing. Untying her mule, she looked wistfully up the hill at the trees that might be lying on that pile above the Gayheart homeplace if only Joel Martin could get the faintest idea of what she and Peter were trying to do.

"I don't guess 'twould be any harder to git this business

through Betsy's head than through a head like his," she said to herself as she rode along. She might better have stayed in her cabin and spent the morning weaving. The trouble was that the people who were interested in a neighborhood cabin had no logs to spare, and the people who lived back where the wood had not all been cut off could not possibly understand why there was need of such a cabin.

When toward noon Lona rode up Hollybush, she did not look in the direction of the log pile but kept her eyes fixed straight ahead.

Meanwhile, Peter's morning on upper Hollybush had been equally disheartening. Joe Slone told him, "We got a schoolhouse. What do we want a neighborhood cabin fer?"

"This is a kind of school," said Peter, "a school to teach the young people to earn a better living than they can get hoeing a little corn and raising a pig or two. And there's no room for workbenches and pottery wheels and looms in the schoolhouse."

"You kin have my barn fer your school," offered Joe, pointing to a log building about the size of his cabin. "My mule Lizzie'll keep ye comp'ny, tee-hee-hee-hee! Mebbe you kin learn her somethin'."

"Much obliged," said Peter soberly. "I've got a barn of my own and a mule too. Neither your barn nor mine is big enough for this purpose."

"'Tain't big enough to dance in. I reckon that's what you-uns want."

There was a dogged set to Peter's jaw as he rode past what he called the "Hollybush woodpile." Eph Hall had promised one log, more to get rid of him than because he was interested in the cabin. Otherwise, his morning's ride and his long talks had borne no fruit. Well, they could get enough logs for a good-sized weaving cabin for Lona, anyway, he decided, and he might have to work for another year in his barn. Lona

"Wal, I don't guess I'd miss a couple more o' them hickories."

must not know how discouraged he was beginning to feel. He was going to keep on campaigning for contributions—if it took years to get enough logs. That afternoon he would write a letter, telling about his plans for the cabin and what such a workshop would mean to Hollybush, and he would send it to people he knew in the level country and ask them if they wanted to be shareholders. Surely this appeal would bring in a few dollars, and even a little money would buy several logs at Hollybush prices.

Dick, too, noticed how slowly the donations of logs were coming in. He was also conscious of the fact that Lona had ceased to chatter gaily about the results of her trips on Betsy. Without mentioning the fact to either Lona or Peter, he enlisted in the campaign.

Thus it came about that after Eph Hall had gone through one of his annual winter sieges of bronchitis and had recovered with Dick's help, he hailed Peter one day from his cabin door with a "Hey, Buddy! You recollect I done promised you a log fer that-thar cabin you aims to build?"

Peter nodded, certain that the old man was going to prove to be an Indian giver.

"Wal, I don't guess I'd miss a couple more o' them hickories. That'd make three."

Peter never knew that the two logs were really Dick's gift, that they took the place of a fee for his services to Eph. Neither did Lona suspect that Joel Pease's sudden decision to give one log was due not to her own persuasiveness on her third visit to his cabin, but rather to gratitude for relief from an aching tooth.

So the winter wore on. The log pile grew slowly, and the spirits of Lona and Peter went up and down with alternating hope and discouragement. Yet neither shared the discouragement with the other. Only the hopes were shared.

Chapter 30

The Cabins That Grew

Redbud time had come again. In the weaving cabin, a strip of cloth in Lona's loom glowed against the dull background of time-darkened logs, as bright as the blossoms on the ridge. "There," said Lona as she unrolled the shining homespun, "that's one done." She took it over to the only window in the cabin and held it up so that the sunlight shone through the bright-colored folds.

The colors of redbud, of new grass, of pine-tree bark, and of soft gray moss were in those threads. "Oh!" she exclaimed out loud. "It's beautiful." Not since the weaving of the "Forty-nine Snowballs" had she felt such delight in her work.

"Come see my curtain," she called to Sairy Ann and Mammy Hall, who sat talking together on the porch of the Hall cabin while Gail and Dicky played on the floor. "It's a pine-tree pattern," Lona told them as they admired it. "See, there's the tree and there's the roots down below the brown needles. I'm a-going to take it down-creek to the new cabin now and see how it looks at the winder."

She started down the steps, then stopped. "Aunt Sairy, can't you leave Dicky and Gail here and come with me? You ain't seen the cabin since Peter laid the floor and made it look fine-pretty inside."

Hand in hand, they went down the trail, skipping from stone to stone in the creek like two children, till they came to where a new cabin perched on the hillside. From within came the sounds of hammer and saw.

"Oh! It does look like a homeplace already," said Sairy as Peter and Pappy Hall appeared in the doorway to welcome them.

"Ain't that a right smooth piece o' floor?" asked Pappy proudly as he drove a nail into a loose board.

"Smooth! Why it's a regular dance floor," said Peter. "Swing your partners!" he called out, taking first Sairy's arm and then Lona's in an impromptu reel.

"Now, Aunt Sairy, look yonder and see what Peter carved," said Lona, when they stopped for breath.

Sairy Ann gave an exclamation of pleasure as she stood before the fireplace and looked at the procession of mules Peter had cut into the wooden mantel.

"Over there," went on Lona, pointing to the side of the chimney, "he's a-going to build a cupboard, and you'd oughter see the chair he's a-making down in his shop, and the andirons and candlesticks."

Suddenly remembering the reason for her visit, Lona unfolded her curtain and held it up to a window. The sun, shining through the bright cloth, made a rosy pool of color on the floor, like the reflection of a stained-glass window.

"There just never was anything so fine-pretty ever made before," declared Peter with fervor.

"Looks like the sunrise," was Pappy's comment.

Lona fairly crowed with delight. "Oh! I didn't reckon there'd ever be another homeplace as pretty as the house on the ridge," she exclaimed to Sairy Ann, "but this one's a-going to be, sure."

"It's a-going to be prettier," said Sairy. She thought back to the time when she and Dick had built and furnished the house on Wildcat Ridge and decided that she had not spoken the truth. So far as she was concerned, no house, no matter how pretty its curtains and its carved mantel, could ever compare to that homeplace of hers and Dick's. "May you both love this house and be as happy in it as Dick and I have been in ours," she added almost solemnly.

"And now," suggested Peter, "let's go up and inspect the big cabin." Farther up the ridge and a few rods up-creek rose a limestone chimney, and around it, the walls of a log cabin were slowly rising. At one side lay a pile of logs ready to be laid in place.

"Howdy," called out Bud Hayes and Mark Gayheart, putting down their hammers and looking proudly around, as though it were their own house and they were showing it off.

"You two worked out your time long ago," said Peter. "You won't have any crops this year 'cepten weeds if you don't stop."

"Mary and Lizzie said they'd do extry crop-hoeing if we'd keep on a-workin' down here," explained Bud.

"Bless their hearts," said Lona. "After the working a week from Saturday, I don't guess there'll be much left to do; seems like every man and boy anywhere around was coming."

Peter grinned. "Maybe they have seen the chickens Sairy Ann is fattening for the dinner and the big ham Mammy Hall is going to bake."

"And the spiced peaches Lizzie is a-getting ready," added Lona.

Peter stood by the pile of logs and looked on them with smiling satisfaction. "I can almost tell where each one of them came from. Those hickories are Lish Reynolds'. They grew on the top of Hog Mountain, and it took three afternoons and two plugs of tobacco to get Lish to see that there was any sense in building this cabin."

"Reckon he sees sense in it now," interrupted Mark. "He worked here all day yesterday."

"Those two straight poplars are Bud's," went on Peter, "and those shingles over there were growing on Breakneck Mountain two weeks ago."

"Clippety-clop!" sounded along the creek below as Twinkle and the doctor came riding home. "Yoo-hoo! Uncle Dick," called Lona. Dick threw the bridle reins over a young dogwood and climbed the hill to the cabin. "These two cabins just grow like corn overnight," he declared.

"They're a-growin' by the power o' this here right arm, and o' Mark's and young Peter's," said Pappy Hall.

"And if everybody will just keep well tomorrow, my right arm is going to help it grow," promised Dick.

They walked up the creek trail together, Sairy Ann, Lona, and Dick, who led Twinkle by the bridle. Lona did most of the talking. She was so excited and happy over the future homes of the Peter Gayhearts and the Allen-Gayheart Industries that neither Sairy Ann nor Dick had a chance for more than a word or two now and then.

When they came to Preacher Johnny's cabin, the old man hailed them from the door. "I got something to show you two." He pointed to Sairy and Dick. "Lona, she can't see it yet." Lona grinned understandingly and went on up the trail.

"How's that fer a table?" he asked them, pointing to the middle of the kitchen floor. "I don't guess her and Peter will need any dishes. They kin put their victuals right on that and eat offen it, if they wants to, and they won't git no splinters into their fingers, noways." He smiled at his little joke and ran his hand over the smooth top of the table he was making. It was of sycamore wood, almost as white as marble, and the preacher had planed and polished it until it was as smooth as marble.

"That's as fine a table as I ever saw anywhere," said Dick, with genuine admiration.

"And as fine a wedding present as any bride anywhere ever had," added Sairy Ann.

Chapter 31

The Working

Lona added a crusty drumstick to a pan full of fried chicken and covered it with a cloth, singing softly—

> *"We'll kill the old gray rooster*
> *When they come,*
> *When they come."*

Meanwhile, Sairy Ann, with lightning-like movements, was pulling brown-capped biscuits out of the oven and replacing them with fresh tins of snowy dough.

Dick stuck his head in the kitchen door to report, "There's such a crowd down there it looks like a funeral meeting. Everybody came that was asked and a sight of folks that weren't. Some came to work, and some came just to eat. But Peter has set them all to doing something—even the youngsters. He's a wonder. That boy ought to be the boss of a big construction company."

At that moment, Lije, who had not been seen since he went to bed the night before, came running down from the top of the ridge with a pan in his hands. "Lookit! Lookit!" He pointed to the dark brown, sticky mass in the pan. "I knowed fer weeks there was a heap o' honey in that thar tree yonder, but I didn't cut it down till this mornin', so's to save it fer the workin.'"

"Wild honey! What could be nicer with biscuits!" exclaimed Sairy Ann as she took the pan from Lije. "The bees on this ridge might as well give up trying to keep their sweets as long as you are around."

Lije grinned. "And I gits there 'fore anybody else," he bragged.

A clump-clump of hoofs and a dull scraping sound announced the arrival of Pappy Hall, with Blackbird harnessed to a large box on wooden runners. "I kin pack your victuals down to the workin' along with Mammy's, if you has them ready," he announced, taking long, appreciative sniffs and lifting the white cloths from the pans of chicken and biscuits. "That'll eat good," was his comment on the contents of each one. At sight of the wild honey, he stopped short and almost dropped the load he was carrying to the sled. "Where'd you find a bee tree?"

Lije pointed up the ridge. "Yonder by the big rock."

Pappy looked disgusted. "The bees must tell you where they are a-goin' to live." He was a "bee liner" of long practice, and he hated to see Lije beat him to a bee tree.

"I tell you what I think, Pappy," said Lona. "I think Lije tells the bees where to hive, and they do just like he tells them."

Dick had not exaggerated the size of the gathering at the new cabin. The hillside echoed to an orchestra of hammers, saws and axes, and men, women and children were as thick as ants on an anthill. "Just see all they got done," exclaimed Lona, hardly believing her eyes. "They're putting on the roof, and it ain't dinnertime yet."

Sairy Ann, Mammy Hall, and Lona joined the women and girls clustered about the board tables that had been set up in front of the cabin. "Hope we has enough," said Mammy doubtfully. "They'll be hungry as houn' dogs."

Lona of Hollybush Creek

Granny Slone, in her Sunday black dress and her best white sunbonnet, went about, looking over the food, taking sly tastes here and there and asking questions of everyone who had time to talk.

By twelve o'clock, the hastily built tables threatened to collapse under the load of good things to eat. Every cook had been afraid she would not have enough and had cooked more than she had agreed to. Dick called the crowd to the feast with a mighty shout, and before the echoed "Dinner!" had died away, every hammer was still. The women and girls rushed about, filling coffee cups and keeping the pans of food in circulation.

It "ate better than a foot-washin' dinner," in Preacher Johnny's opinion, and no higher praise could be given on Hollybush Creek. The annual foot-washing ceremony which the church held every summer was a time when the women outdid each other in bringing the best they could cook.

Not till the men had finished and were sitting under the trees chewing tobacco did the women and children have their turn. The size of the men's appetites had worried some of the boys and girls. "Was there any more chicken?" they asked each other, as the pans went up and down the tables, growing lighter and lighter with each trip. With pathetically anxious faces, they watched the bowls of golden spiced peaches pass from hand to hand. "Ain't ye a-going to leave nothin'? Ain't ye a-going to leave nothin'?" little Jimmy Boleyn cried out as he saw Bud Hayes help himself to his tenth biscuit. Jimmy was calmed only by being shown the baskets and kettles of food held in reserve for the second table.

It was midafternoon before the tables were cleared and the leftover food and the dishes packed up. Hollybush women had few chances to get together and talk. They were making the most of the opportunity the working dinner gave them to gossip and had no intention of going home till it was time to milk the cows.

Lona stole away from the chattering group and went by herself down to the little cabin that seemed to be inviting her to come and see it. Already it was a little like her own homeplace. She closed her eyes and saw chairs and tables in their places and her fine-pretty curtains at the windows and a bright fire burning on the hearth. She saw Peter and herself sitting by the fire together and smiled at the picture, then suddenly grew sober. In so short a time now, she must leave the house on Wildcat Ridge, leave Sairy Ann and Dick and Gail and Dicky and Lije. To be sure, they would visit back and forth, but never again would she be a part of that happy household. Well, it was up to her to make this house a place like the house on the ridge, where happiness seemed to glow as brightly as the fire on the hearth and to warm the hearts of those who came through the door. She vowed to herself that, with Peter's help, she would not only make her home such a place but that the neighborhood cabin as well should give comfort and cheer to Hollybush.

"They told me you were lost, and here you are right at your own homeplace and smiling as though you had the pleasantest thoughts for company."

Lona came back from the future with a start at the sound of Peter's voice. "I have," she said. "I am imagining what it will feel like to live here."

"That's a thought that makes me smile, too."

When they got back to the "big cabin," they found only a few stragglers left. These were gathering up nails and hammers and unhitching their mules. Last of the guests to leave was Preacher Johnny, who, as a carpenter, seemed to feel that the "working" was his special responsibility. "They done worked good," was his verdict, pronounced as he shouldered his axe and cross-cut saw.

"Yes, they done worked good," Peter repeated the old man's words, as he took a last look with Lona before he "packed" her home on his mule.

"Didn't you git plumb discouraged, Peter, when we were trying to git enough lumber fer it?"

Peter nodded. "For a while, I figured we'd have to give up building a big cabin like we aimed to, that we couldn't get enough logs for anything more than one room. But I didn't tell anybody, and we've done it some way; I don't just know how."

"It took a sight o' mile-riding and talking," said Lona, "but I'm glad we didn't give up. And it was fun, too—at least some of it was fun."

Peter lifted her up onto his mule's back, swung himself into the saddle in front of her, and started up the trail for Wildcat Ridge. "Yes, it was fun," he agreed emphatically, "and there's more fun ahead."

Chapter 32

A "Big Time" on Hollybush

Granny Slone brushed her thin hair back from her forehead till it shone like white satin. She patched a hole in her best black dress and hunted in her bureau drawers till she found a yellowed white muslin collar.

At the same time, Mammy Hall, looking as excited as a girl, was putting on the new dress Sairy Ann had made for her and looking timidly at her reflection in a cracked looking glass. "Seems like it was right-smart lively fer an old woman," she said to Pappy, but she was thinking that she looked rather well in the dark blue silk with its sprigs of bright flowers.

In Preacher Johnny's cabin, Maria was trimming the old man's hair and snipping bits of down off his neck. "Why can't ye sit still?" she complained. "You're as fidgety as a flea-bit dog. If you ain't careful, I'll be cuttin' a piece outen your neck."

"I'm afeerd I'll be late," fretted the preacher. "Bud Hayes done rid by half an hour ago."

Up on the ridge, there was so much excitement the house would have rocked if it had not been built on strong foundations. "This suit is so tight I feel like a mummy," said Dick as he got into his best serge suit for the first time in over a year. "Say, are you the bride, or is Lona?" he asked Sairy Ann when she tied his necktie. "You look so pretty in that blue dress, Preacher Johnny will make a mistake and be marrying you over again, if you don't keep out of his way." Sairy replied to this compliment with a kiss and began brushing Gail's bright ringlets.

Meanwhile, Lona was standing on tiptoes to see as much as possible of herself in the small looking-glass above her bureau, patting a rebellious curl into submission on her forehead and poking and pulling nervously at her white dress. "How do I look?" she asked when Sairy Ann came to see what she could do to help her.

"Beautiful," said Sairy, and she meant it.

The simple dress Lona had made for herself. Her bride's bouquet of pink laurel had been gathered on Wildcat Ridge. She wore no veil. Yet she was far lovelier to see than many a lace-veiled, satin-gowned bride.

"Bije is waiting," called Dick. Lona gave a last look into the glass. Sairy Ann adjusted Dicky's socks and retied Gail's shoes. Lije swung himself down from his loft room, looking uncomfortably dressed up. They started down the ridge path to where Bije and his mules waited. Sairy Ann went ahead with wedding cake Number One. Lona followed, holding Gail's hand and carrying her bouquet. Lije was third in line, bearing wedding cake Number Two as proudly as though he had baked it himself, and Dick brought up the rear with Dicky riding on his shoulder and chattering gleeful nothings.

The jolt wagon had been washed and equipped with kitchen chairs especially for the wedding party. They all managed to climb up over the wheel without damaging best shoes or clothes and to keep their chairs from lurching and hurtling them into the creek during the brief drive to the neighborhood cabin.

While the Lawrence family had been jogging down-creek, Mattie Boleyn, Lizzie Gayheart, Mary Caudle, and Holly

Reynolds were scurrying about the cabin, massing laurel blossoms above the fireplace, making one corner into a bower of laurel and ferns, and setting great jars of flame-colored wild azaleas on either side of the door.

Bije pulled up the mules with a "whoa-a" that could be heard halfway to Bull Creek and helped his passengers down with a flourish. The cabin overflowed with men, women, children, and babies. They sat on the doorsteps and under the trees. Hollybush people had not seen such a "big time" in years. They were celebrating two important events—the opening of the new neighborhood cabin and the marriage of Lona Allen and Peter Gayheart. No wonder that everyone came who was invited and that many others who scarcely knew the bride and groom found it necessary to ride their mules to the mill or the store that afternoon.

When all the guests had had a chance to inspect the weaving room and the workshop, Dick stood up on the doorstep so that those both indoors and out could hear him and began to talk. He started with Mammy Hall's old "kivers" and the linsey-woolsey cloth Aunt Sally had woven and made into a suit for Uncle John years ago—a suit that Uncle John had never been able to wear out. The magic practiced by Aunt Betsy with roots and bark in her black dye kettle figured in Dick's speech. So did Lona's prize "kiver" and the loom that had traveled from the level country to the mountains. He grew eloquent about the tirelessness of Lona and Peter in reviving the old forgotten handicrafts, teaching them to the young people, and finding buyers for their work.

Finally, he told how the new cabin had grown log by log, then paused in his story to hold up dramatically a large, framed sheet of paper headed, "Shareholders in the Hollybush Neighborhood Cabin." "Amos Boleyn—three logs," he began and went through the long list that ended—"Esra Slone—two days' work." Then he stepped into the cabin and hung the document over the fireplace.

Now came one of Preacher Johnny's prayers that was twice as long as Dick's speech. When he had finished, Lona started the old hymn she had sung so often at her loom. One by one, other voices joined with her sweet soprano—some young and piping, some old and quavering, until there rose from the hillside a great chorus declaring—

> *"With perfect delight,*
> *By day and by night,*
> *This wonderful song I'll sing."*

By the time the last echoes had died on the hilltop, Lona and Peter were standing together in the corner of the weaving room against the bank of laurel and ferns. Those outside crowded up to the windows and door while Preacher Johnny began the ceremony. He ended with another prayer, not quite as lengthy as the previous one. The first to kiss the bride were Sairy Ann and Mammy Hall. Then Grandma Gayheart put her thin arms around Lona and "thanked God that she had been spared to see this day."

Now Mammy Hall and Sairy Ann were bringing out from concealment the two enormous cakes and setting them on the table under the trees. Peter's mother and sister-in-law, Lizzie, appeared with pots and pails of steaming coffee, while Lona cut the cakes and Sairy Ann and Dick began to pass them around, making sure that Grandma Gayheart had the first piece of one cake and Preacher Johnny the first of the other.

Lona's cake was not a wedding cake at all. That is, it was not the rich, fruity mixture baked for such occasions in the level country. But it had a sprinkling of raisins in it, which caused much excitement among the children, and even icing—another rare treat for Hollybush. There was enough for everybody—though the pieces had to be small—and enough to serve the fringe of onlookers down by the creek, many of whom had brought their own refreshments in the form of moonshine.

Like most Hollybush parties, this one did not break up until milking time. Before the last mule had plodded down the hill, Sairy Ann and Mammy were on the ridge, cooking the wedding supper, to which, beside Lona and Peter, only Grandma Gayheart, Peter's father and mother, Pappy Hall, and Rachel were invited.

It was a merry supper party. Mammy, recalling the confessions she had listened to in the weaving cabin, beamed with pride on the bride and groom. Grandma Gayheart's eyes were almost as bright as Lona's. Sairy Ann and Dick grew sober at times when they remembered that Lona was leaving them. But they kept their feeling of loss to themselves. Lona could not bear to think that Wildcat Ridge was no longer her home. She thought instead of the new house with bright curtains and new furniture that waited down yonder for her to make it a home.

It was dark along the creek trail when Lona and Peter made their way to the little cabin. To their surprise, a welcoming light shone from the windows. Lizzie and Mark had lighted a lamp and left it to cheer their homecoming. They crossed the threshold almost reverently, and a smile of contentment was on their faces as they looked around. There wasn't a pleasanter place than this anywhere, Lona decided. No "store-bought" furniture could compare with these pieces put together in Preacher Johnny's kitchen and in Peter's barn workshop. Her curtains, the colorful cushions she and Sairy Ann had made, the big living room rug that was Holly's wedding present, and her prize "kiver" in the bedroom, were all the more cheerful for their background of logs and unpainted boards.

"It's simply beautiful," said Lona.

"It is," agreed Peter, "and it's our own homeplace."

He knelt on the hearth and lighted the fire that was already laid, partly because the summer night was cool, and partly because it was a fitting rite for the beginning of a home. The flames leaped up and sent out a glow that seemed to give life to the cabin.

Explorations revealed gifts they had not discovered earlier in the day—jars of Mattie Boleyn's spiced peaches on the kitchen table, a baked ham, a cake, and a big pat of fresh-churned butter in the kitchen cupboard.

When they had investigated and admired every corner of the house, they sat down by their fire and talked of all the things they were going to do together on Hollybush Creek in the years ahead.

Lona looked up to the mantel, where the little wooden cat Peter had carved for her sat looking serenely down on them, as though pleased with its new home.

"There's our mascot," she said.

THE END

More Books from The Good and the Beautiful Library!

The Story of Marco
by Eleanor H. Porter

Up From Slavery
by Booker T. Washington

Nearby
by Elizabeth Yates

*The Story of
John Greenleaf Whittier*
by Francis E. Cooke

www.thegoodandthebeautiful.com